Asking for a Friend

Kate Mallinder lives with her husband, four children and two cats near Ashby-de-la-Zouch in Leicestershire. She grew up in Solihull and went to college in Leeds. She's currently studying for an MA in Writing for Young People at Bath Spa University. She also enjoys doing school visits and leading workshops. Her first book, *Summer of No Regrets*, was published by Firefly in 2019.

Firefly Press and the author would like to thank Inclusive Minds (www.inclusiveminds.com) for introducing us to Ella Sanderson through their network of Inclusion Ambassadors. We are very grateful to Ella for her helpful advice.

Asking for a Friend

Kate Mallinder

Firefly

First published in 2020
by Firefly Press
25 Gabalfa Road, Llandaff North, Cardiff, CF14 2JJ
www.fireflypress.co.uk

A CIP catalogue record of this book is available from the British
Library.

ISBN 9781913102296
ebook ISBN 9781913102302

This book has been published with the support of
the Welsh Books Council.

Typeset by Elaine Sharples

Printed and bound by Pulsio Sarl.

*To all the writers who think this
could never happen for them*

And this includes my younger self

CHAPTER 1

I missed having her around. My sister, that is. It wasn't like I couldn't live without her. I was still here, breathing and everything. But the world didn't feel right.

I walked up the school-bus steps and went to sit in my usual seat. Hattie wasn't there yet. Rummaging through my bag, I found my phone. Instagram first. There was Rose. She looked happy, smiling in at the camera, a council ID badge on her jacket. It made my stomach hurt.

I looked out of the window as the bus swung out and onto the road. The grey, drizzle-soaked streets of Manchester rumbled past. I'd been travelling this route since I started at Caldy High School. Some days there was more rain, some days less, but that was about it. I like that it doesn't change. Change makes my fingers twitch and everything feel wrong.

It wasn't a 24/7 feeling – missing her. There were chunks of the day where I didn't even think about Rose being 185 miles away in Weston-super-Mare. A lot of the time I'd forget that it had been 21,167 minutes since I'd last seen her. And I only checked on her social media at eight set times of the day.

Mum says, 'Change is inevitable, you've just got to get used to it,' but I don't agree. This wasn't inevitable. It was Rose's choice. She'd got a job and moved out and I wasn't going to 'just get used to it'. At least it wasn't forever. She'd be home soon. I just had to hang on to that. Should I perhaps count down until I next see her? I bet there's an app for that.

'Hey, Agnes, are you even listening to me?'

I looked up from my phone.

Hattie was glaring at me. 'You're not, are you?'

'I... um...' I hadn't even noticed her sit down next to me.

She rolled her eyes. 'Never mind. It wasn't important anyway.'

This is one of my least favourite things people

say (and, yes, I have a list). Was it *really* not important? In which case, great. We can both save the time and energy of a conversation. But what if it actually *was* something important? And she was just *saying* that it wasn't. I got this wrong with Rose once and she didn't speak to me for a whole day. But my point stands. It's not my fault if she doesn't say what she means.

'Well, if you change your mind, and it is important, please tell me.' I nodded and tried to look interested. Hattie has a gift for talking. I don't always have the matching gift of listening. But I like Hattie. Mum calls her my bus buddy.

'Guess you haven't heard then? That answers my question.'

I was about to ask what she meant when a boy yelled from a few rows back.

'Oi, Hattie, good weekend? I heard I missed a *great* party.'

I didn't know the boy, and Hattie hadn't been in school yesterday, so I assumed it was one of her circle of popular mates catching up with her. Hattie didn't reply though. She just stared at her phone. She wasn't even scrolling. Perhaps she hadn't heard.

At the next stop a girl bumped Hattie on the way past.

'Watch out,' said Hattie, rubbing her arm.

'Sor-ry,' said the girl. 'Didn't see you there.'

Which was odd. Because she's hard to miss is Hattie. It's the hair. Brown curls to her shoulders which she never ties up. She's got a really big smile too. Though she wasn't smiling then.

'People can be such idiots,' she muttered. Was she speaking to herself? Was this a rhetorical question or was she expecting me to answer? I searched her face, trying to decide.

I had no clue. But I did have something to say.

'Most people can be. Idiots, I mean. You've got to ignore them.' I had plenty of experience.

'Easy for you to say,' said Hattie, focused on her phone.

Why was it easy for me?

'It's getting easier,' I said. 'Ignoring those "Oops, sorry, did I bump you?", "Oops, sorry, did I laugh at you?", "Oops, sorry, did I make fun of you in front of the whole class?" You've got to ignore and move on. What's the alternative?'

Hattie was looking at me now, frowning a bit. 'Huh. I guess so.'

'Anyway, this is my stop.'

The brakes squealed as the bus slowed down. Kids pushed and shoved to get off first. I stood back from the scrummage knotted around the door. There was nothing to be gained by being seventeen seconds in front. I stepped down off the bus right foot first. It was raining properly now. I pulled up my hood and walked along the pavement avoiding the cracks. Hattie waved through the window. She always did that. I nodded in reply, not wanting to get my hand wet by waving back.

I unlocked the front door. The house was silent. Mum wouldn't be in. I closed the door and let the air whoosh out of my lungs. After being with people for hours, this moment on my own was my favourite bit of the whole day. School gives me a serious social hangover. I hung up my bag and draped my coat over three pegs so it'd dry properly. I got my Tuesday snack of peanuts and lemonade, then went upstairs. I stopped outside Rose's bedroom. The door was shut.

Why couldn't it go back to how it was? There were jobs here in Manchester. Rose could have got one of those. I missed her face. I missed how she stacked the dishwasher (especially now Mum's doing it). I missed her lasagne on Thursdays. I even missed her singing in the shower – something I *never* thought I'd miss. I know having Asperger's makes me react really strongly to change, but knowing that

5

doesn't help. Seeing Rose, having Rose home, getting everything back to normal; that would help.

I walked into my room and sat down at my desk. Perhaps I should tell her. Perhaps she would come back sooner if I did. Holding my phone up, I leaned my elbows on the desk.

Me: *I miss you.*

She replied almost immediately.

Rose: *I miss you too.*
Me: *Why don't you come home then?*
Rose: *Lol, I've only just got here.*

She hadn't. It had been two weeks.

Today was Tuesday. We broke up for Easter on Friday. If she wasn't coming back for a visit, perhaps I could go to her. It wouldn't be the same, but at least I'd see her face.

Me: *Can I come to stay? It's the holidays next week.*
Rose: *That's a lovely idea, but now's not a great time.*
Me: *Why not?*
Rose: *It just isn't. I've got stuff going on.*
Me: *Like what?*

Rose: *Stuff. How about you come and stay in a few weeks' time?*

Me: *I've got exams, remember?*

Rose: *Crap, I'd forgotten. After that then?*

I counted up. That would be two and a half months away. But she'd be back by then, surely? The two months would be up.

Me: *Won't you be home?*

There was a pause. She'd read my message but wasn't replying.

Me: *Rose? You'll be back, so I can't come and see you after my exams. Next week is the only time.*

Rose: *I really do miss you and Mum, Agnes. It's just this next couple of weeks are really full-on. You understand, don't you?*

I'm not sure I did. Something felt off but I couldn't work out what. And, besides, I wouldn't stop her from doing anything. I wouldn't be any bother. I just wanted to see her. And maybe get her to make me some lasagne.

I could go anyway. Just to see her. It was ages

until after my exams and I wasn't sure I could last that long.

If I *were* to go to Weston, I would need somewhere cheap to stay, and also a cheap way to get there. Rose was sleeping on a friend's sofa, so I couldn't stay with her. I didn't even know where that was.

Me: *What's your address again?*

Rose: *You're not coming OK? I love you, but next week is really important for me. I'll see you soon, I promise.*

She knows me too well.

Me: *Oh hahaha. I might be wanting to post you something.*

Rose: *But you're not, are you? Nice try, Agnes. Love you x*

Humph. I went back to googling places to stay.

Usually, if I needed to talk to Rose, I'd just walk into her room and she'd be there, working on her laptop, or watching a movie. I didn't like that I couldn't do that anymore. I don't get why she had to leave and mess everything up.

Of course, there might be a reason. I know I

misunderstand sometimes. I do that. But rather than explain, people talk about sticks. As if *that* helps. 'Agnes, you've got the wrong end of the stick *again*,' they say, and roll their eyes, as if what they've said was obvious, and I am an idiot.

I am not an idiot.

I pulled up a map. How would I get to Weston? I knew it was by the coast. They say sea air is good for you. I'd eat more fish there too. I could totally load up on brain food before my exams. So many good reasons to go.

I traced round the coast, past Anglesey, and down the west coast of Wales, then back in past Swansea and Cardiff, along the other side of the Bristol Channel, past Clevedon until my finger stopped at Weston-super-Mare. Maybe coach? Perhaps train?

Hang on, hadn't Hattie been there sometime recently? I vaguely remembered her going on about it on the bus. She might have useful information.

I found her number on the geography WhatsApp group and called her. She answered almost immediately.

'Agnes? Is everything OK?'

'Yes. Why wouldn't it be?'

'Only you have literally never called me before.'

'I've never needed to.'

There was a pause.

'What do you want, Agnes?' She sounded a little terse.

'Weston-super-Mare? You said you went there on holiday? I don't remember the details.'

'Yes. Last summer.'

'That's interesting.'

'Look, Agnes. What's going on? Why have you called about my holiday from eight months ago?' She paused. 'You know what they say, a problem shared is a problem halved.'

I had never found this to be true, except maybe with Rose. But Rose wasn't here.

'Come on.'

I paused for a second. 'I need to go to Weston next week,' I said quietly. 'And I wondered if you would recommend it?'

'I would recommend Spain,' said Hattie. 'Or France, or America, or Devon, or Scotland, or pretty much any other place on earth.'

'It's not a resounding endorsement.'

'No,' said Hattie. 'Though the problem was probably more to do with being with my annoying brother than the place itself.'

'Ah.' Well, that wouldn't be my problem. My sister isn't annoying.

'Seriously, Agnes. What's going on? You never go anywhere, and now – what? You're planning to go to Weston? Just before your exams?'

'It's nothing. Don't worry about it.' I went to hang up.

'Don't you dare hang up on me, Agnes.'

What was she? Psychic? Then I realised I needed to lie. Hattie needed an explanation. She wouldn't be able to bear not knowing, so I needed to tell her something – anything.

'I need to go somewhere quiet for the holidays so I can get some revision done. That's all. No drama.' I crossed my fingers behind my phone as I held it. 'And I just wondered where you stayed.'

'Why didn't you just say so? My aunt has a bed and breakfast. Awful place. No one needs that much floral fabric. But she cooks a mean breakfast.'

'Fuel for the day,' I murmured.

'What?'

'Nothing. Would she be OK with me staying? I mean, on my own?'

Would anywhere take a sixteen-year-old on her own?

'Maybe,' said Hattie. 'But I've just had the most *brilliant* idea.'

'Really?' I felt doubtful.

'I could come too! Think of it, just the two of us. Paddling in the sea, playing the arcades on the pier, eating candyfloss. It would be great fun.'

I was about to shut her down.

'And because it's my auntie's place, we'd stay for free.'

For free. No money needed at all. I couldn't say no.

'We would have to do revision as well,' I said.

'Of course.' I could imagine her wafting the idea away with her hand.

I knew Hattie. Once set, Hattie is as unstoppable as the tide.

I sighed. 'OK. Shall we go to Weston together at Easter then?'

There was screaming. I took that as a yes.

CHAPTER 2

Hattie

I hung up, bounced off my bed and ran down the stairs two at a time, landing with a jump that shook the mirror in the hall. Agnes' idea had come at exactly the right time. I needed to escape. The last couple of days had been hell. I'd faked it yesterday to dodge school and I wished I'd done the same today.

'Quietly!' bellowed Dad from his study. I ignored him and ran into the kitchen.

'Well, you looked pleased with yourself,' said Mum, busy peeling potatoes while scrolling a document on the screen propped up on the worktop. 'Which I have to say is a nice change. I was getting a bit worried about you.'

'It's because I've had *the* most amazing idea.' I needed to play this carefully. Mum wasn't massively obsessing about my exams, but if she even got a whiff that this was a holiday, then I could kiss it goodbye. 'It's a study break. Recommended as the best way to prepare for exams.'

I saw Mum's face twitch with interest. Good job, Hattie. But don't blow it now – carefully does it.

Ethan was playing on his Xbox in the corner of the kitchen, headphones on. When I'd come in, he'd flicked them back, so one ear was out. That kid really needed to mind his own.

'Studies show that going away from home a few weeks before exams can help to recharge pupils, and boost immunity.' I was in serious blagging territory now. 'Of course, I would still be doing plenty of studying, *obviously*. But a change of scene can aid revision, helping key facts to stick. It's new research – location association.'

'Don't fall for it, Mum,' said Ethan, his eyes not moving from the screen. Even his tone was irritating. All sing-song and goodie-goodie. I needed to rise above it. I needed to be mature enough to ignore my blister of a brother.

Mum looked worried. 'We can't go anywhere at Easter. Dad's got his big project happening. Though, I agree, that does sound like a good idea.'

'*Well*,' I said, limbering up. 'I could go to Auntie Sadie's and stay with her.'

'What? You can't do that. It's not fair.' Ethan was the one irritated now.

Mum frowned a little. 'On your own?'

'Of course not. My friend would come with me.'

'She doesn't have any friends,' crowed Ethan. 'Not after that party,' he mouthed at me. Mum's focus was still on the potatoes. I flicked a couple of fingers his way, trying to style it out. How the hell did he know about that? Or perhaps he didn't actually know, had just heard a rumour and presumed. I cringed at the thought of all of the rumours that absolutely must be going around. James shouting on the bus had proved that.

Mum's face was flashing through a rainbow of emotions. She finally picked one. 'A friend?' The selected emotion was undeniably 'hopeful'.

'Yes.'

'Not one of the unholy trinity?' Mum had no time for Scarlett, Chelsea and Zara. And that was without her knowing the latest.

'No.'

Her eyes narrowed. 'Not a *boy*friend?'

'Mum!' I had to shout over Ethan's laughing. 'No, her name's Agnes, and we want to go somewhere quiet where we can do lots of studying, but also have a break before the exams.'

'You've not mentioned Agnes before.'

'Haven't I?'

'No.'

'She's on my bus. I sit by her every day. So … can I call Auntie Sadie and ask?'

Mum finished peeling a potato, rinsed it and added it to the pan. I let her think. I'd learned it wasn't any good rushing Mum. If you pushed, she would close it down. My finger picked away at a bit of loose skin on my thumb. Ethan and I waited, hoping for exactly opposite outcomes.

'OK,' she said. 'Ask Auntie Sadie, but if she says no, or she's fully booked, then that's that. No trying to go somewhere else. You're really too young to be going off by yourself.'

'Noooooooo!' howled Ethan. 'Mum, that's not fair.'

'Yes, Mum. Of course. I'll ring her now.'

I grinned at Ethan before skipping off upstairs, my socked feet skidding on the polished floor. I crashed into the hall table and bumped hard against the wall.

'Quietly!' shouted Dad, from behind the closed door. 'And stop that hullabaloo, Ethan. Life's never fair.'

I took the stairs two at a time. Our stairs are a satisfying depth.

Auntie Sadie answered after three rings.

'Hello, Bayview Bed and Breakfast.'

'Hi, Auntie Sadie. It's Hattie.'

'Hattie, darling! How are you? It's been ages since I've seen you.'

'I'm all right, thanks. I've rung to ask a favour.'

'Anything for my favourite niece.'

I giggled. I am her only niece.

'Could me and my friend come and stay next week? For a study break? I know it's really short notice.'

'That would be wonderful. I've just had a couple of cancellations, so I'll block out a room for you. What fantastic news!'

'Thanks. I knew I could count on you.'

I could hear Auntie Sadie's grin when she answered. 'You can always rely on me. Let me know when you're arriving at the station and I'll come and fetch you.'

When I came off the phone, I texted Agnes: *It's ON! Auntie Sadie has got us booked in. A week by the sea, here we come!*

I smiled to myself, enjoying the tingle of hope that was spreading through me. I hadn't felt that since before Saturday night. And Ethan was right. Not since that party. Not since that kiss. I shuddered at the memory. It would be good to be away. Away from annoying brothers, away from my silent friends, and away from Manchester. Perhaps, when I got back, everything would have sorted itself out. It would be old news by then. And while I was away, I would make sure they'd all see what an amazing time I was having without them. Weston would shine on Instagram.

Agnes was replying.

I've drawn up a list of jobs that need to be done before we go. Perhaps you would like to do roughly 50% of them. I'll email the list. It's only eighty-four hours until we leave and there's lots to do.

I read the text twice through. Then an email pinged into my inbox. *To do list.* I scanned down it. There seemed to be a lot of unnecessary ones like 'ensure that we both have a new set of highlighters for revision notes'.

I texted back: *I'll get snacks. You sort how we get there.*

That should do it.

This was just what I needed. A complete break. It all felt such a mess. The three people I thought I could trust above everyone else had turned on me.

Since Saturday, they'd not said anything nasty. They'd just not said anything. They were ghosting me. But they'd clearly said stuff to other people. Other people who I wished would ghost me rather than say what they'd said.

I knew it wouldn't help, couldn't help, but my fingers took me there anyway, finding their Instagram, making me look at their perfectly poised pictures. If that party hadn't happened, I'd be part of that group now, not here at home, trying hard not to cry.

If you wished hard enough, could you undo the past? I had really tested that out. What I wouldn't give to go back and redo that evening. I wouldn't have even stopped to chat to Bailey, let alone gone outside with him or sat next to him. Had I led him on? I hadn't thought so, but maybe I had. Maybe talking to a boy gives him the wrong idea. Maybe having a laugh with him was the wrong thing to do. Maybe just being there had been wrong.

CHAPTER 3

Jake

Two weeks ago, I changed seats on the bus. I couldn't deal with all the team chat at the back. I had something else on my mind and what felt like a permanent headache. And talking about strategy every waking moment didn't seem, I don't know, relevant somehow. Like I'd suddenly got a glimpse of what life was all about and now the routine chat, that a few weeks ago I'd happily be joining in with, left me cold. It no longer mattered. A day after that, I came off the team. They'd assumed it was exam pressure and I let them think it.

Since then, I'd sat in a different seat. No one came to sit next to me. I was behind two girls, also in year eleven, and every day I pretended to be listening to music when really I was totally eavesdropping on their conversation. It started the day I left my phone at home. I scooched right down low in my seat, aiming for invisibility. The two girls in front of me were the usual two. I hadn't paid that much attention before.

'You know Mr Dalglish?' said the girl with dark-brown curls. 'Old jackets, weird moustache? Well, he had a massive strop yesterday. He wanted me to move desks. No idea why. But I didn't want to move desks. I was by the window, and I'd worked hard to get that seat.'

There was a murmur from the other girl. She was white, with hair that was always pulled into a ponytail.

'I had to literally fight Stephanie Brown to get it. So I emptied my pencil case out on my desk and moved each pencil, pen and rubber separately. That's when he sent me out. Can you believe it?'

'Why did he want you to move desks in the first place?' asked the other girl.

'Dunno. Though I missed what he was talking about before, so that might have had something to do with it.'

'I get sent out all the time.'

'Do you? I didn't think you were the type?'

'There's a type?'

'Course! The rule-breaker sort. You seem to me to be a rule follower.'

'I follow my rules,' said the other girl. 'They don't always match with theirs.'

'Fair enough.'

The school bus had pulled in by then, and they got off ahead of me. I realised the journey had flown by, without any of my usual thoughts. For ten whole minutes I hadn't had to listen to my brain churning over and over. Since then I've always put one earbud in and had my music on low. I don't listen in a creepy way, don't get me wrong. They're just interesting. It's not that they even say anything shocking. It's normal, everyday, uncluttered, and it takes my mind off … stuff. The more I listen to them, the more I can't help myself. I've got to know quite a bit about them now. Mostly about Hattie. She's the chatty one. Agnes is more often quiet, nodding along to Hattie's chat. Between you and me, I don't think she's always listening that hard.

This morning was different. They were both talking at the same time. I shuffled in my seat to hear them better.

'So that's accommodation, study aids, snacks and transport sorted. Just need to clarify on the survival pack.'

'I've told you, we don't need one. It's only Weston, not Kathmandu.'

'But what about Kendal Mint Cake? We definitely need that.'

'Surely that would come under snacks.' I'd spoken without thinking.

They both turned to look at me.

'Well, I mean...' I could feel the heat rising up my neck. 'It is something to eat.'

Hattie narrowed her eyes. 'Who asked you anyway? Didn't anyone ever tell you it's rude to listen to other people's conversations?'

I nodded. I knew I mustn't give away I'd been listening to them for nearly two weeks.

'Sorry,' I stuttered, picking up my phone and pretending to scroll.

'He does have a point,' said Hattie. 'If we included that in the snacks list, we could leave off the emergency needles and anti-malaria tablets.'

I raised my ears without raising my eyes.

'I guess,' said Agnes.

'Hey, have you got a name?' said Hattie.

I risked a glance up. Hattie's face was squished between the two coach seats in front, her eyes on me.

'Erm, yes. I'm Jake.'

'Well, thanks, Jake. You solved a problem we've

been discussing for more than twelve hours. Felt more like three days.'

'It's actually been only ten hours and thirty-six minutes,' came Agnes' voice.

I grinned. 'You got some plans then?'

Hattie nodded and pulled her head back a bit to include Agnes. 'We're going on holiday, just us, to Weston.'

'It's a study break. For revision,' said Agnes.

'Whatever. We're away from home, friends and families – if you don't count my Auntie Sadie – for a whole entire week in the Easter holidays.'

'Really? That sounds amazing. Other than the revision bit. Obviously.'

And I meant it. Really meant it. I realised with a big whoosh that I would give anything to go with them. Avoid the thinking. But there was no way, of course. And there was no way I could suggest it without coming across as out-and-out weird.

'Got any plans other than revision while you're there?' I asked.

Agnes said, 'No, not really,' at exactly the same time as Hattie said, 'Loads.'

They looked at each other.

'What do you mean?' demanded Agnes. 'We're there to revise.'

'Well, of course, that's what I've told my mum,' said Hattie, laughing. 'But we can't only do revision. We'd burn out. Don't want to peak too soon and bomb our exams.'

'I don't think that's actually a thing. I'm pretty sure the more revision you do, the better grade you get. It's a direct correlation.'

'I have no idea what you're talking about,' said Hattie.

'Perhaps if you did a bit more revision, you'd know,' snapped Agnes.

They were both quiet.

'I guess I can always go off and do my own thing when I'm done revising but you haven't,' said Hattie.

'That would work.' Agnes nodded.

'Doesn't sound much like fun doing stuff on your own,' I said. After this last two weeks, I should know.

Hattie looked at me. She had dark brown eyes and I couldn't quite read her. Was she mad because I'd butted into their conversation again?

I shrugged. 'But it doesn't.'

'You're right,' said Hattie. She was chewing her bottom lip.

'But it definitely beats staying round here. I'd

give anything to be going on holiday. Seriously. You've no idea.' I hadn't meant to say that.

Hattie's eyes narrowed. The bus swung into the school. She didn't say anything else, which wasn't like her. She put her phone into her bag. She and Agnes left the bus, but I sat a bit longer, thinking. Perhaps a break from Manchester was a good idea. Take my mind off stuff.

Once the bus had pretty much cleared, I stood up and swung my bag onto my shoulder. Hattie and Agnes had got it sorted. I longed to run away somewhere, just escape. Perhaps I should. Just run and run and run until everything, my family, my friends, my thoughts were all left behind. Trouble was, I'd still be taking my problems with me.

CHAPTER 4

Agnes

When I got on the bus after school, Hattie was already in our seat. She was literally bouncing up and down.

'What's wrong with you?' I slid myself onto the velour seat. She carried on wriggling around. I frowned at her.

'I've had an idea. And don't say no straight away.'

'Go on.' At least she was expecting a no from me.

'I wondered. Seeing as you're going to be revising all the time. And I want to do a bit of revision and a bit of having fun…'

'Revision can be fun, you know,' I said.

Hattie rolled her eyes. 'Whatever. I wondered if we should invite someone else along. So I've got someone to hang out with when you're still deep in your books.'

She was doing the classic wide-eyes technique, combined with a hopeful smile. I wasn't moved. I wanted to say no. I was only going with *her* because of the free accommodation, though I knew this wasn't a good thing to say. However. My brain gnawed at the problem. It could actually be quite helpful. If Hattie was occupied, I could go and see Rose.

'Let me think about it,' I said.

Hattie squealed and looked like she might hug me, but thankfully thought better of it.

Jake walked up the aisle and plonked himself down behind us. I'd never really noticed him before. He had dark brown skin, dark eyes and a non-school-regulation hoodie. He seemed nice, so I nodded at him. He grinned back. Was more social interaction now needed? I couldn't tell, so opted for not and went back to Hattie's question.

'Do you have anyone in particular in mind?' I asked. If it was that awful Stephanie Brown, it was going to be a hard no.

Hattie came really close. I could smell her chewing gum. 'I wondered about Jake.'

What? The boy sitting behind us? But we'd hardly spoken to him.

'Why?'

Hattie grinned. 'Well, he looks fun, and he really wants to go away for Easter. And I think he has a nice smile.'

'Ted Bundy the serial killer had a nice smile,' I muttered.

'What?'

'Nothing.'

'And don't forget,' said Hattie, 'he does have exceptional skills. He sorted out our emergency supplies list. No messing.'

She had a point. He had. But we hardly knew him. Though he would be an excellent distraction for Hattie, if I wanted to go off on my own without explaining where I was going. Which was the whole point of going.

'He might not want to.'

'Let's find out,' she whispered back.

'Hey, Jake...' She grinned at me, then turned round to look between the headrests.

'That's me.' Jake pulled an earbud out of his ear.

'So I was wondering. Would you fancy coming with me and Agnes to Weston-super-Mare during the Easter holidays?'

'This is not a definite offer,' I said, pushing Hattie to one side. 'We're just canvassing interest.'

Jake was wide-eyed, looking from me to Hattie. 'Err, what?' he said.

He'd heard.

'Would you. Like to come. With us. To Weston?' I repeated, in a clipped voice.

Jake grinned. 'I heard. What, do you want an extra person to split the bills?'

Hattie shot me a look and pushed me away from the gap. 'I thought it would be nice to have someone to hang out with when Miss Study-Pants over here is revising. Like you said, it sucks to be on your own.'

Jake was clearly thinking fast. 'Sure. Sure, yes, that would be great.'

Hattie grinned at me.

'So, Jake,' I said, ignoring Hattie, 'now we've confirmed you are interested, we have to check that you are suitable.'

Hattie and Jake's smiles dropped in synchrony.

'What the heck, Agnes?' said Hattie.

'For all we know, Hattie, he could be a mass murderer. No offence, Jake…'

'None taken.'

'So we have to ascertain whether he's likely to murder us in our beds.'

Hattie's eyes nearly disappeared, she rolled

them that hard. 'Well, you'll have to do me too then.'

'Don't need to. I've been analysing you for years.'

Weird, but Hattie didn't seem to like this.

Jake, though, was up for it. 'Ascertain away, Agnes. I will answer anything you want to know. You can't be too careful these days.'

I smiled smugly at Hattie. 'Thank you, Jake, for understanding.'

Hattie looked exasperated.

'OK. Tomorrow after school,' I said. 'Both of you come to my house for psychoanalysing. And I'll dig out my lie-detecting kit.'

CHAPTER 5

Hattie

I waved to Agnes as she walked back past the bus window.

'She's quite quirky, Agnes, isn't she?' came Jake's voice from the seat behind.

'You can say that again,' I said, twisting in my seat. 'But she's all right. Once you get past, you know, everything.'

Jake laughed. He had a nice laugh. Uncomplicated.

'So, which stop's yours?' I asked. I couldn't get over the fact I'd not clocked him on the bus before. Guess he wasn't one of the shouty, 'look-at-me' crowd.

'The one after yours.'

Huh. So he knew which stop was mine.

'How come the two of you are going to Weston

together? If you don't mind me saying, you don't strike me as best buddies.'

'How would you know?'

I watched the red blush rise from his collar, burning through his dark brown skin. How *did* he know?

'Just a hunch.' He wasn't looking me in the eye, even though my head was pretty much jammed between the headrests. 'You seem quite different?' It was more of a question, than a statement.

I took pity on him. He was glowing now.

'I guess,' I said. 'Agnes said she wanted to go to Weston, and my auntie has a bed and breakfast there, so it's kind of just happened. I mean, we are friends.'

I think. What is friendship exactly? We shared our lives for a total of forty minutes per school day. That's got to count for something. Come to think of it, I didn't know all that much about Agnes. She didn't give much away.

'Perhaps we all ought to do the psychoanalysing she's got planned. That way we all know what we're letting ourselves in for.'

Jake snorted. 'I'm not sure Agnes would like that.'

I laughed too. Though maybe she would. She'd be able to analyse the group dynamics.

At my stop, I pulled my bag onto my shoulder, said, 'See you tomorrow,' and got off the bus. Walking back home, it felt weird to have two new people to think about. Two people I had said 'See you later' to. Nearly balanced out the three who still weren't speaking to me.

The front door banged against the wall, before I slammed it shut.

'Quietly!' yelled Dad from his study.

I dumped my bag, kicked off my shoes and went in search of a snack. This was a lottery. All depended on where in the shopping cycle we were. For the day or two after Mum had been to the supermarket, the shelves were piled high with tasty snacks, but by day six, things could be looking fairly bleak, with only the out-of-date raisin bars left, right at the back. Not even extreme starvation after fish on Fridays could tempt me to have one of those.

Ethan gets home before me and was already wired up to the Xbox, a range of half-eaten snacks around him. He'd better not have eaten them all. I was in luck. I grabbed a bag of crisps, quietly pinched a chocolate biscuit from Ethan's pile (he's totally oblivious when he's screened up) and retreated to my room.

Should I tell Mum that Jake may be coming with us? I remembered her boyfriend comment and cringed. She would totally see this the wrong way. But I would have to tell Auntie Sadie – he'd need somewhere to stay. Maybe I should wait until after Agnes had psychoanalysed him, but it might be too late by then. I decided to ring.

'Hello, Weston's best bed and breakfast,' came Auntie Sadie's voice.

I laughed. 'Hi, Auntie Sadie.'

'Gorgeous! How are you? All set for your trip? Have you rung with the train times?'

'Well, yes and no,' I said. 'We get into Weston at three on Saturday.'

'Smashing. I'll be there to pick you up. And what else was there?'

I paused, not quite sure how to put it. 'Can you keep a secret?'

'Do I run a bed and breakfast?'

'Ummmm,' I said.

'It means, yes, I have to keep everybody's secrets.'

'Oh right. Of course. OK, then. Could someone else come and stay too?'

'No problem, I'll just put up an extra bed in your room.'

'Well, I, um…'

'Not like you to be lost for words, honey pie.'

No, it wasn't.

'The thing is, it's a boy. Who's coming with us. Maybe. Agnes hasn't analysed him yet.' I cringed.

'A boy, eh? Does your mum know?'

'Crumbs, no! She would Freak Out. But there's nothing going on. Honestly. He's just a…' I paused. 'He's a friend.'

Auntie Sadie chuckled. 'Well, as long as you all behave yourselves, and don't upset my regulars, I have no problem with *A Boy* coming along too. I take it I'm not to mention this to your parents?'

'They wouldn't understand.' And they really wouldn't. They'd immediately jump to the conclusion that I liked him. But I didn't. Not like that, anyway.

'No problem,' said Auntie Sadie. 'Your secret's safe with me. Now, let me see, which room to put him in? Ah yes.' I could hear her turning over the crackly pages of her large desktop diary. 'The attic room is lovely. Great sea views. He'll like it up there.'

'Wonderful,' I said. 'And Auntie Sadie?'

'Yes?'

'Thanks for being awesome.'

'Can't help what I am.'

Once off the phone, I scanned through Instagram. A photo of Zara, Chelsea and Scarlett came up. 'Chilling with the gang' was the caption under it. A pain stabbed my heart.

We'd done it to other people in our group before – the ghosting thing. Usually there was a good reason to cut a person off. Rachel had decided to join a different group. Stacey had complained about Zara to the head of year. I guess mine had been The Kiss.

I switched off my phone. I wanted to say 'Who needs them anyway?' but who was I kidding? I'd been friends with Scarlett, Chelsea and Zara since we'd met in year seven. We'd spent every lunchtime together. I'd hugged Zara as she cried about her parents' divorce. We'd laughed at Chelsea when she cut her fringe too short, but defended her when anyone else tried it. Scarlett and I always shared our homework, and often it was chatting over problems with her that made things clear. I couldn't believe they'd ghosted me. I thought our friendship was stronger than that. What stung the most was that they hadn't believed me. They'd believed someone else instead. And that hurt. That hurt like hell.

CHAPTER 6

Jake

I was nearly out the door, when I called back to Mum. 'I'm out tonight, after school.'

Mum appeared in the hallway, cup of coffee in her hand. 'Really? You haven't mentioned it?'

I was sure I had. Well, pretty certain anyway. 'It's no big deal. Just a friend's house.'

'OK,' said Mum. 'Which friend?'

'No one you know.'

Mum frowned. 'Why's it such a big secret?'

'No secret. Just me, going round to a mate's house after school. No biggie.'

'Whose house, Jake?'

'Fine! I don't know why it's so important. Her name is Agnes. I'm going to her house. There's a few of us going. We're going to revise. Happy now?'

'Lovely. Don't know why you didn't just say that.'

'I've got to go. I'm going to miss the bus.' And I slammed the door shut behind me. No point in telling her about the trip. Or the lie-detecting test.

That afternoon, the bus squealed up to Agnes' stop. My regular headache now had a matching stomach pain. Just low level but still there.

'Follow me,' said Agnes. She sounded even more uptight than usual. Perhaps she was having second thoughts about asking me round.

'Are you sure this is OK?' I asked.

'Why wouldn't it be? I suggested it, didn't I?'

I held my hands up and let her walk on ahead of me. She was going to be tricky to spend a week with if she was always so prickly.

Hattie fell into step beside me.

'So, what's her house like?' I asked, finding it hard to imagine her anywhere other than the bus.

'Dunno. Never been.'

'What?'

'I know. This is a big deal. For her, I mean.'

I nodded.

I watched Agnes walking ahead. Was she wondering why I wanted to go with them? What tests was she going to ask me to do? Was I going to have to tell them the truth about why I wanted to get away? I hadn't told anyone.

It was two weeks ago that my world tipped. I'd found something in the shower. A lump. Down there. I tried not to think about it. It was probably nothing. It'd clear up on its own. Probably. Nothing to worry about. And yet my brain wouldn't leave it alone. Even though I kept telling it, pleading with it to stop thinking, the thoughts kept coming. Brains, it turns out, scream worse-case scenarios at you. What if it's really bad? What if it's cancer? What if it's spread? What if the headache and stomach pain is proof that I'm riddled? What if ... it kills me? I felt like I was about to jump off a bridge on a bungee rope the whole time. I couldn't sit still for long. Couldn't settle at anything. Nothing distracted my mind. If only I could just get my brain to stop freaking out, I'd be sorted.

I'd checked again this morning. The lump was still there. So it hadn't cleared up on its own.

'OK, this is my house,' said Agnes. Her face looked strained. I think she was trying to look welcoming but failing horribly.

'Nice one,' I said, trying to help her out. I know what it feels like to be awkward.

'Hope you've got good snacks,' said Hattie, as she went inside ahead of Agnes.

'Of course,' said Agnes. 'It's Thursday, which means popcorn and milk.'

I stifled a laugh.

Agnes shot me a look. 'If you wanted something else, perhaps you should've brought something. It is customary to bring a gift for your host.'

Was she for real? Agnes is hilarious.

'No, popcorn and milk sound great.' I smiled at her.

She nodded, seeming satisfied with my answer.

Agnes' house was small, neat and impossibly tidy. She led us through a dark hallway to the kitchen at the back of the house. There was a small table with three chairs and a selection of stuff on it, all lined up in neat rows – a pad, three pencils, a list and some medical stuff. I recognised one was a blood pressure monitor. I'd watched my fair share of spy movies to know what one looked like. Agnes hadn't been joking. This was a literal lie-detector test.

'I thought we'd do the test here,' she said.

'Snacks first,' said Hattie. 'I'm starving.'

Agnes walked into the kitchen, leaving me and Hattie standing in the doorway. She pinged popcorn in the microwave and measured out three equal glasses of milk.

I raised my eyebrows at Hattie and she widened her eyes back.

Agnes brought the milk and popcorn to the kitchen table. 'You can sit down, you know.'

Awkwardly, I scraped out one of the chairs and sat. The silence was unbearable.

'So, who else lives here?' Hattie looked around.

'It's just me and my mum,' said Agnes, eating the popcorn in pairs.

'So why three chairs and three mugs hanging up by the kettle? And I spotted a picture of you and two other people in the hall.' Hattie seemed quite observant.

'My sister, Rose,' said Agnes. 'She used to live here. But she doesn't at the moment.'

Hattie looked like she wanted to ask more.

'Shall we start then?' said Agnes, clearly changing the subject.

'Yes.' I nodded. 'I'm keen to be wired up and told when I'm lying.'

Hattie grinned. Agnes remained emotionless.

'This is no joking matter. Remember, we're here to establish whether or not you are suitable to come to Weston with us.'

She fastened the blood-pressure band around my upper arm, another band around my wrist, and picked up her pencil.

'Crumbs, Agnes. You're not going to accidentally electrocute him, are you?' Hattie stared at all the wires and battery packs. 'How does this work?'

'I ask him a few questions, stuff we already know the answers to, just to calibrate. Then we ask him stuff we don't know the answer to. I'll be measuring any changes in blood pressure and heart rate.'

Hattie nodded.

'Let's start. And don't keep interrupting, Hattie, you'll mess up the results.'

'Yes, boss,' Hattie muttered under her breath.

I was pretty sure Agnes heard her.

'First question,' said Agnes. 'Is your name Jake?'

An easy one. Jake is my name. Not short for anything.

'Yes.'

Agnes checked the readings on the two monitors and wrote some things down.

'Second question – do you go to Caldy High School?'

'Yes.'

More scribbling.

'And the third test question. Do you get the bus to school?'

'Yes.'

'Now for the real thing. Have you ever injured someone?'

I thought hard. I wanted to answer no. Obviously. I'd never injured anyone on purpose, but last summer I did accidentally smack my cousin in the teeth with a bat playing French cricket on the beach.

'Yes,' I said.

'Really?' asked Hattie. 'You know that doesn't sound great.'

'Accidentally.'

'Quiet, please,' said Agnes, her face giving nothing away. Hattie leaned forward, as if I was the most fascinating lab rat she'd ever seen.

'Have you any criminal convictions?'

Phew. An easy one.

'No.'

I couldn't help grinning.

'Do you fancy Hattie?'

'What?' Both me and Hattie spoke at the same time.

'What's that got to do with anything?' asked Hattie, her face pink.

'I agree,' I said.

Agnes shrugged. 'It would make for an extremely awkward week if you did.'

Hattie's eyes were wide.

Agnes said, 'Please just answer the question.'

'OK. No. Sorry, Hattie.'

'No need to apologise,' said Hattie. 'I can't believe you asked that, Agnes.'

'We needed to know. Right, final question. Are you in good health?'

Good health. What is good health exactly? I'm here, I go to school, and to most people I look totally fine. And if I answered no, I'd have to explain. I took a deep breath and tried to think calming, heart-rate-reducing thoughts.

'Yes.'

Agnes checked her results, wrote them down and looked up at me.

'So?' asked Hattie. 'Did he pass?'

'Apart from blatantly admitting to injuring people, yes,' Agnes said, still not looking away. Had she guessed?

Hattie whooped. '*Yes*! Weston here we come – only one more day of school, then we're off to have a week of fun … um … revision,' she corrected, catching Agnes' eye.

CHAPTER 7

Agnes

I had sent seventeen messages to Hattie and Jake and had exactly zero replies. Honestly, whoever named it *social* media obviously didn't know people like this.

I tried again.

By now you should have your bags packed. From a health and safety perspective, your luggage shouldn't weigh more than 15kgs, as we're going to have to lift it from platform to train several times during the journey. I have packed all relevant text books, and I thought we could visit the local library should we require background reading. My bag weighs 14.9kgs.

I wasn't stupid. I wasn't expecting a reply to this. But I did feel oddly disappointed. Which is a funny feeling to have when I had zero expectations.

My phone pinged. It was Hattie.

You've packed already? You legend. I've not even started. What do we need again?

I kneaded my temples with my knuckles. I had sent a packing list, broken down by sections – clothes, course texts, study aids, snacks. Surely she would realise her error? Surely?

I lasted thirty-seven seconds before I replied, tagging in the packing list.

A helpful list, so you don't forget anything. Only 12 hours till we meet at the station.

Hopefully that would focus her mind.

Cheers. Loads of time then.

I couldn't handle it. I put my phone on charge and left my room. Hattie would do what Hattie would do. Best not to witness it. It would Stress. Me. Out.

Mum was in the kitchen, her shift over. She was buttering toast, and a mug of tea was steaming next to her plate.

I didn't know what to say, so I didn't say anything. Neither me nor Mum are big chatters. That was more Rose's thing. Now she wasn't here, it felt really quiet. Which is usually a good thing: quietness. But this quietness felt odd. Like I only realised when we had a power cut just how much noise the fridge made. Well, that's Rose. She's a background noise that feels odd now she's stopped.

Mum took a big bite out of her toast and chewed. She hadn't reacted to me going away for the holidays, only asked who I was going with, where I was staying and if I needed any spending money.

Of course she hadn't reacted to me saying I was going to Weston, because I had told her I was going to Blackpool. Then if I managed to get Rose to come back home it would be a surprise. Think she'd like that. And I definitely would. If Rose came home everything would feel right again. I'd got Rose's address from Mum. It was easy. Just told her I wanted to send Rose a postcard from Blackpool. Simple.

'You all packed?' Mum asked, after a second bite of toast.

'Yup.'

'Got all your revision stuff?'

'Yup.'

'Of course you have. I don't know why I'm checking really. Habit, I guess.'

I nodded.

'You know I can't take you to the station tomorrow?'

'I'm getting the forty-three bus. It'll take twenty-nine minutes.'

Mum nodded. 'Good.'

She slurped her tea. It was obviously still too hot.

'Who is it you're going with? I know it's Hattie – who was the other?'

I sighed. I had already told her. 'They're both from my bus. Hattie and Jake.'

'And they're ... all right, are they?'

'Yeah. They're fine.' Which wasn't untrue. They were fine. Whether I'd still think that after a week in their company would be another thing. I was beginning to feel quite jittery about spending all that time with them. I was sharing a room with Hattie. At least at home Mum respected a closed bedroom door and didn't bother me. I didn't think Hattie would have the same boundaries.

'That's good,' said Mum.

The smell of the toast was making me hungry, so I put two slices in and pushed the lever down.

'I will miss you.' Mum was looking into her cup of tea. 'You know, while you're away. The place won't feel the same without you.'

She looked up and smiled a little at me.

'I'll be back though,' I said.

49

'I know.'

I didn't really get it. It wasn't going to be forever. And she'd have the place to herself. She could do whatever she liked.

'But you're going to have an amazing time.' She sighed. 'I remember when I was your age. Everything just felt so ... so possible. Like my whole life was in front of me, just waiting to be lived.'

It was clear Mum was having one of her overly emotional moments. Just nod and smile. Always worked.

For the record, I absolutely did not feel like that. I felt stressed that I had forgotten something and that I only had 0.1kg of luggage space to play with; that I was seeing my sister in a town I'd never been to, while spending a week with two people I didn't really know all that well. And, on top of all that, it was only five weeks until my GCSEs. Which felt, quite honestly, like the least of my worries.

But I didn't tell Mum that. I just nodded and smiled.

'You trust me,' said Mum, lifting her mug up. 'You're about to have a holiday where the memories will last a lifetime.'

Huh. No pressure then.

After I'd finished my toast, I walked down the

road to the newsagent's on the corner. The bell above the door jangled as I pushed it open, and the smell of sweets and newspapers hit me, a sickly, inky smell. But I wasn't going to be deterred by a smell.

I checked the community noticeboard. The square of paper was still there. I pulled it off and took it with me to the counter.

'Excuse me?'

The woman behind the till looked up from the *Racing Times*, pencil in hand.

'Is this job still available?'

The woman peered at the paper I held out. 'Too right,' she said.

'And can anyone apply?'

The woman laughed. 'I'm sat here for more than twelve hours a day, seven days a week. My bum's now flat I'm sat down so long.'

I wondered why she didn't stand for a bit, if that was a concern.

'I'd take a literal monkey, if it applied.'

'Is that a yes?'

'Yeah.'

'I know just the right person. Could you hold the position for a week?'

The woman laughed, which turned into a hacking cough.

'It's first come, first served. Though that ad has been there two months, so I reckon you're safe. Pin it back up on your way out.'

I walked over to the board and held a pin between my fingers. The woman went back to her newspaper. I stuck the pin in the board. And the advert in my pocket.

CHAPTER 8

Hattie

It was a beautifully sunny morning. I could see Agnes and Jake waiting for me on the platform opposite and I had a clear two minutes before the train arrived. I had nailed this!

I kissed Mum quickly.

'Don't worry, Auntie Sadie is collecting us from the station.'

Agnes was waving, and I was uber-aware that Jake was sat right next to her. Mum still knew nothing about Jake, and I literally didn't have the time to explain.

'You don't have to wave me off,' I said, willing her to leave.

Mum looked towards the platform, then back towards the car. She'd parked on double yellows.

'I'm fine. Honestly,' I said. 'You can text whenever you're missing me.'

Mum smiled and hugged me. 'Be safe, OK? Have an *amazing* time.' She squeezed extra hard on the word amazing.

'Of course,' I said as she let go. 'It's pretty much guaranteed with a study break.'

She laughed. 'And yes, please do *some* work.'

Which made me wonder how much she knew.

Out of the corner of my eye, I could see Agnes was off the bench now and pretty much dancing in her effort to get me to the platform before the train arrived.

'I've got to go.'

Mum hugged me again. 'Have fun.'

I took a photo of the station and uploaded it to Instagram, trimming Agnes off the edge. *Holiday here I come.*

I walked through the barriers and made my way up and over to the opposite platform. I looked across the tracks. Mum hadn't moved. If she got a parking ticket, it would be all her own fault.

'Jake!' I called, keeping my eyes on Mum and not looking sideways at him. I was pretty certain Mum could only see us, not hear us. 'Stay over there, OK?'

'What?'

'Just do it!'

I glanced across at him. He had stayed on the bench. Agnes was next to me but that didn't matter. It would have been odd if she wasn't. From Mum's point of view.

I turned back to Mum and waved. 'Wave at my mum, would you?' I said to Agnes.

We both stood and waved.

'Think the train's coming.' Agnes looked down the track.

'Oh, thank goodness for that.'

The train pulled in, blocking Mum's view.

'Come on, Jake!' I called. 'This is us.'

He hadn't heard me. He was just sat, staring into the distance.

'Jake!'

'Huh?'

'It's our train! Come on!'

'OK, right.'

Jake and I heaved our bags up the two steps onto the train. Followed by Agnes.

Agnes was eyeing us up. 'You didn't follow my packing instructions, did you? Those bags are way heavier.'

'It's fine.' I wheezed dramatically and strained to lift my bag.

Jake chuckled. Agnes rolled her eyes.

We pushed our bags into the luggage rack and got seats around a table. I waved one last time to Mum, as the train pulled out of the station.

'Phew,' I said, dropping my hand. 'That was close.'

Agnes was frowning at me.

'What?' I said. Surely I hadn't broken another one of her rules?

'What was close?'

Ah.

'I haven't told Mum that Jake's coming with us.'

'You didn't?' Both Agnes and Jake reacted.

'She's so uptight about that sort of thing, and I didn't want to have to explain.'

'But it's going to be ten times worse if she ever finds out,' said Agnes. It's annoying how right she was.

'I know. Which is why she can never know, OK?'

Jake was grinning.

'What's so funny?'

'Just didn't think I was the kind of boy you'd keep secret from parents, that's all. Reckon I need to revise my image.'

I laughed. 'Yeah, you're a real wild one. So, you told your parents, right? What did they say?'

Jake smiled. 'It's Mum and my stepdad, and they were totally fine with it. Wanted to know everything about you both, of course, but no problem.'

'You tell them about the lie-detector test?' I challenged.

'No!'

Both Jake and I laughed. Agnes was looking between us, as if trying to work us out.

'But you just said you told them everything,' she said.

'Everything they needed to know.' Jake grinned. 'There's a difference.'

Agnes nodded. 'Ah, got it. Yes, that's what I did too.' She seemed pleased to have un-puzzled our conversation. 'I told my mum we're going to Blackpool.'

That made both me and Jake howl with laughter.

'What?'

'That's loads worse,' said Jake.

'Why?' said Agnes. 'It's just a lie, just like yours.'

'Don't worry about it,' I said. 'Anyway, I'm starving. Who brought the snacks?'

'That was supposed to be your job.' Agnes looked my way.

'Was it? Oh crap. I forgot.'

'Luckily, I've got back-up snacks.'

She produced a flask of tea and three packets of Skips. Her Saturday snack, evidently.

'What is it with the snacks?' asked Jake. 'Have you got like set snacks for set days?'

'Yes,' said Agnes. 'It makes sense, doesn't it? Varied diet, saves time decision-making and you can plan ahead. I'm always surprised more people don't do it, to be honest.'

Jake put a Skip on his tongue and thought for a moment.

'It's OK,' said Agnes. 'You can say it. I know most people don't think like me. I have Asperger's. What's logical and sensible to me, isn't always the same for others.'

'Actually, I was just thinking when you put snack planning like that, it does actually make sense,' said Jake.

'Just most people can't be bothered,' I said.

Agnes shrugged. 'Doesn't seem like a great reason not to do something though, does it?'

We changed trains without any bother and basically munched and chatted all the way to Weston.

'Exactly on time,' said Agnes, approvingly, looking at her watch.

I bit my lip. I'd told Auntie Sadie we got in at three. And it was only two-thirty.

We stood at the station's entrance, with our bags heaped next to us. There was a gentle mist drizzling, slowly soaking us. I took a selfie, with the ornamental station in background. *Vintage Weston – love it.*

'What does your aunt look like?' asked Jake.

'Like this.' Agnes thrust a photo of my aunt from about thirty years ago in front of us. 'I got it off the tourist information website.' She saw our expressions. 'What? I do my research, OK?'

I was going to have to come clean about her not getting here until three, and that she didn't look anything like that picture, when a small minibus pulled up in front of us. The window wound down.

'All right, my munchkins?' It was Auntie Sadie. No need to fess up now.

She switched off the engine, put her hazards on and got out. 'Figured you'd be on this train,' she said to me. 'There wasn't one arriving at three.'

Agnes frowned at me. Yeah, cheers, Aunt S.

She was dressed as wackily as ever. She is what my mum describes as a 'splash of colour'. Every colour. Including a new hair colour: vivid purple.

She gave me a massive hug. 'So good to see you, gorgeous girl.'

I hugged her back.

'And you must be Agnes?'

Agnes put her hand out to shake, but Auntie Sadie pulled her into a massive hug. Agnes looked shocked.

Jake got the same bear-hug treatment, before we loaded our bags into the back of the van and got in.

Agnes was chatting to Auntie Sadie about meals and menus, which made a ton more sense now I knew Agnes had Asperger's. I checked Instagram. There were loads of new photos of Scarlett, Chelsea and Zara. They looked like they were having an amazing time. Seeing them really didn't make me feel great, so why did I keep looking?

I'd really dropped off posting. I mean I still was, but I didn't like to admit that there wasn't as much going on. Not since I'd been ghosted. And my likes were way down. But that was going to change. This week was going to be amazing. I looked out of the minibus window. We were driving along the seafront now. The mist was rolling in off the sea and up and over the sea wall. There was hardly anyone about. Unless I could get an arty shot of the pier disappearing into the mist, this was not a good day to start Instagramming again.

I flicked back to Scarlett's account: picture after picture of her and Bailey came up, their arms wrapped round each other, gazing into each other's eyes. There was even one of them eating spaghetti like they do in that Disney movie.

My stomach knotted again, making me want to double over a bit as I scrolled. I couldn't look at Bailey. Memories of the party made me shudder. I'd been sure no one had seen. It had been an awful thing, but I'd walked away as fast as I could. I'd thought that would be it. That it would be over. But Sharleen must have seen. Bailey wouldn't have told anyone? Surely he wasn't that stupid? But what those photos shouted at me was that Scarlett believed Bailey, believed Sharleen and didn't believe me. That's the bit that hurt the most, like I'd been punched in the soul.

CHAPTER 9

Jake

Hattie's Auntie Sadie was bonkers. But she was so friendly and chatty that it was impossible not to like her straight away. You could see that Hattie was her niece. Same directness, same 'it'll all be fine' look on life.

The purple hair was a surprise, if I'm honest. And I reckon I counted at least five piercings.

She was being quizzed by Agnes in the front seat, who was trying (I think) to find out whether we're going to get nutritionally balanced meals. She was going on about brain fuel. Auntie Sadie seemed to be keeping up. Agnes had exclaimed twice that her answers were 'excellent'.

Hattie was on her phone again. She didn't look too happy. I wondered why she had to keep checking. I got my phone out and checked her Instagram. Loads of gorgeous photos came up, of the train, our snacks, of her. *Away with friends* read one caption. Weird that she'd not mentioned me or Agnes. Perhaps she couldn't find us to tag us.

It was only about ten minutes before the van pulled up at a row of grey stone houses with big jutting-out bay windows edged with lighter stone. Some had gardens, others had switched garden for parking, but all were bed and breakfasts.

'Here we are,' said Auntie Sadie. 'Bayview Bed and Breakfast – the best in Weston.'

To be honest, there didn't appear to be anything different between Bayview and the rest in the row. Some boasted colour TVs in every room, some en suites. Auntie Sadie's had a collection of garden gnomes gathered around a bench.

'Oh, you've got some new ones!' said Hattie, tucking her phone away.

Auntie Sadie laughed. 'I have. Can't resist them. There's Bob, over there by the wall, and Marcia in the middle. Come on, let's get your bags in. I'll move the van round the back in a minute. Bramble will be delighted to see you.'

We hauled our bags through the gnome garden and into a dark hallway. As my eyes got used to the gloom, a wooden desk came into focus. There were a couple of easy chairs and a coffee table. Auntie Sadie went round the other side of the desk to collect the room keys.

Loud honking came from outside.

'Oh blast,' said Auntie Sadie. 'I'd better move the van. You know where the rooms are, Hattie. Why don't you show everyone where they're staying?'

She dropped three keys into Hattie's hand and rushed out.

'All right, all right, keep your knickers on,' we heard her yell, presumably at the person who'd honked.

Hattie looked around then dropped to her knees by one of the chairs. 'Oh, there you are,' she said. Tucked into the corner, curled up in a large dog bed, was an elderly black Labrador. His tail was thumping against the radiator, with a rhythmic thunk, thunk, thunk.

'Hello, boy, have you missed me? I've missed you. Course I have.'

The Labrador was talking back in small whimpers as if he was actually answering her.

'Jake, Agnes, this is Bramble. Bramble, this is Jake and Agnes.'

I knelt down besides Hattie and patted the dog's huge head. The tail wagging got faster.

'He's lovely,' I said.

'You want to stroke him?' Hattie asked Agnes.

'No, I'm good thanks,' she said.

Hattie gave Bramble a last stroke. 'Come on,' she said. 'I'll show you round. We'll go to our room first.'

She walked down a corridor, passed a door marked 'lounge' and stopped outside a door with a number one on it.

'This is ours, Agnes.'

She unlocked it. Inside was a good-sized room, with two single beds and a horrific amount of chintz. Every surface had a frill. I knew immediately this place would have covers for the spare toilet rolls.

'It's something else, right?' said Hattie. 'Don't worry, you'll get used to it. And after a while, you might even like it.'

Agnes was checking facilities and views and bed squishiness.

'Mmmm, this is good. And a desk for working at. We'll have to have a rota for that, Hattie.'

Hattie laughed. 'There's another desk in the bookroom,' she said. 'I can always use that one.'

'There's a bookroom? Where? What books? Oh, this changes everything.' Agnes was the happiest I think I'd ever seen her.

Hattie grinned. 'Thought you'd like that. Though don't get your hopes up, there's nothing in there that's not forty years old, at least.'

Agnes nodded.

'How about I show you where your room is, Jake, then I'll give you both the tour?'

'Sounds good,' I said.

We went back out into the hall, past the main reception and up some wide stairs. The carpet was uber-patterned and so thick my feet sank into it with every step. On the first landing, a man came towards the stairs. He was tall and was more marching than walking. I'd put a tenner on him being ex-military.

'Good afternoon,' he said, nodding to all three of us.

'Hello,' said Hattie. I just nodded. Agnes ignored him completely.

'It's up again,' said Hattie, starting up the next flight, a bit narrower now, with a steeply pitched ceiling.

'Here you are,' she said as we reached a door with a number 5 on it. She unlocked the door and pushed it open.

The room was different from theirs downstairs. This was light, mainly because of two massive roof lights, and had hardly any chintz, just a solitary overly-frilled ornamental doll in the far corner.

'This is nice,' I said, looking round. Agnes let the door click shut behind her.

'If you stand here, you can see the sea,' said Hattie. 'Well, you can when it's in. It's not at the moment. Though at least the mist's lifting now.'

We stood, looking out over rooftops and a road and the seafront to a vast expanse of grey beach.

'Funny-coloured sand,' said Agnes. 'That must be the mud I've read about.'

'Yep,' said Hattie. 'The beach is good and sandy but further out it's pretty much mud.'

'And the sea's past that?' I asked. I thought I could see a grey line on the very horizon if I squinted.

'Yep. Goes out a really long way.'

'I've read about that, too,' said Agnes. 'It's one of the biggest tidal differences in the world. Which means when the sea does come in, it's really fast.'

'OK, tour time!' Hattie was almost bouncing with excitement.

Hattie and Agnes went out.

I looked out of the window. It was a pretty dramatic view. Not beautiful. But impressive. All that open space before the sea. It had been such a full-on time on the journey, I'd barely had time to think. But now? Now my brain was making up for lost time and it all came crashing back. What was I doing here? Had I really thought I could escape thinking about it all?

Hattie stuck her head back round the door. 'You coming, Jake?'

'Yep, be right with you.'

She left again. I needed to fill my head with other thoughts, other things going on. And right now, having a tour of a chintzy bed and breakfast in Weston was my best bet. I hurried out of the room after Hattie.

Downstairs, Auntie Sadie had finished moving the van and was working through a pile of paperwork behind the front desk.

'Did you find everything OK?' she asked when she saw us.

'Yep, no problem,' said Hattie.

'Well,' said Auntie Sadie, 'tea will be in about an hour. There are only four other guests this week, and they're all out this evening, so that means I get to chat to you guys properly. How about you take Bramble out for a walk up to the Old Pier and back before tea?'

Agnes didn't look so keen, but I was definitely up for having my time filled.

'Sounds good,' I said. 'What's the Old Pier?'

Agnes frowned. 'I'm presuming it's the pier built before the current one.'

Auntie Sadie laughed. 'That's pretty much it. You can't go on it anymore, though, it's not safe, but the walk along the seafront is a nice one.'

It had stopped drizzling by the time we met at the front door. Hattie had Bramble on a lead.

'Are you sure he wants a walk?' said Agnes, looking at him suspiciously.

'He always wants a walk,' said Hattie. 'What, don't you like dogs?'

Agnes wrinkled her nose. 'It's not that I *don't* like them. But I don't *like* them either. I don't *anything* them. I suppose I don't know many.'

'Well, now's your chance,' said Hattie. 'Bramble's a real softie. And he's not going to jump up – he's too old for bouncing. But, you give him some fuss, and he'll love you forever.'

Agnes didn't look convinced.

We started walking along the road, back towards the sea. Within a minute we were looking out over what seemed like miles of muddy sand. The wind was blowing, and I pulled up my hood.

My head still felt sore and I didn't want it to get worse.

The Old Pier was a rusted iron structure stretched between the coast and a rocky island a couple of hundred metres offshore. Back in its day it had clearly been something special – the island had old buildings on it, though most of them had holes in their roofs now. It looked kind of spooky.

'I've always thought it would make a great setting for a Scooby Doo movie,' said Hattie, who had knelt down, scratching Bramble's ears. 'It's like a deserted theme park.'

'It would be perfect,' I said looking out over the mud and water at the pier. 'It's a shame they can't repair it. I'd love to get over there.'

Agnes shook her head. 'No point now there's the new one.'

Which made me feel kind of sad.

As it was only us for tea, Auntie Sadie said we could eat round the kitchen table, rather in the formal dining room. It was warm, and Bramble had settled down in front of the big Aga, his gentle snores getting louder and louder until they disturbed him and he snorted to a stop.

'So,' said Auntie Sadie, pouring us all mugs of

tea and cutting up pizzas, 'what are your plans for the week?'

'Revision,' said Agnes. 'We've got exams in five weeks and we really can't afford to think about anything else.'

Hattie grinned. 'Yes. Absolutely. It's revision every waking moment.'

'Agnes is the really focused one,' I said. 'Hattie and me are planning to do some, but we're going to do other stuff too. Not sure what exactly. But you know more, right?'

Hattie grinned. 'Absolutely. You're going to see all the sights of Weston.'

I smiled. That's exactly what I needed. Lots of things to do and less time to think.

CHAPTER 10

Agnes

My alarm woke me at six-thirty. Hattie's Auntie Sadie had said breakfast would be at eight, and I wanted plenty of time to get ready and review my notes before starting my revision. I figured I could get a few hours done before I went out to see Rose. Rose never gets up before noon on a Sunday if she can help it, so it would be pointless going round before then.

I found my washbag and picked up a pink floral towel.

'What time is it?' muttered Hattie from her bed.

'Just after six-thirty,' I replied.

Hattie groaned. I suspected she was like Rose.

I headed into the en suite and shut the door. The bathroom was a deep sage green, with more pink floral towels and busy wallpaper curling at every corner. It wasn't just the books that were over forty years old.

It took several minutes to work the shower out. There should be instructions on the wall. Why was it always assumed that showers were instinctive?

After my shower, I went back into the bedroom. Hattie hadn't moved. I was about to set up my books on the desk, when I remembered. Mum always goes on about trying to think about other people, trying to see things from their perspective. She says this a lot when Rose is having a lie-in. And Rose, when I've woken her up, says it too. Very loudly.

I didn't want Hattie to have to say anything loudly, so I picked up my bag of study stuff and left the room. Hopefully that was the Right Thing To Do.

I walked along to the bookroom. I would set up before breakfast, then be ready to start the minute I'd finished.

I pushed the heavy door open. The walls were lined with large leather books with small paperbacks crammed into every remaining space. Whoever collected these was a massive Agatha Christie fan.

'Hello.'

I jumped. I hadn't expected anyone else to be in there.

'Don't mind my sister. She never thinks before she speaks,' said another voice.

I looked round to see two identical women in two wingback chairs either side of the fireplace.

'Funny that, neither does mine,' said the first woman.

They glared at one another.

'I've got a sister like that,' I said. They looked at me. They had matching pale-blue eyes, super-wrinkled faces and white-grey hair.

'You have my deepest sympathy,' said the first woman. 'Sisters like that can be a real trial.'

'Tell me about it,' said the other.

I reckoned there wasn't anything else to say. We'd shared the obligatory pleasantries, though granted, they weren't that pleasant. This interaction had set my plans back by a few minutes, so I hurried to the desk and pulled books and notepads out of my bag.

'Who are you? You're not Sadie's niece, are you?' asked the second woman.

'No. She's Hattie's aunt. I'm Hattie's … friend.' Acquaintance might have been more accurate.

'And you're here for a holiday?'

I nodded. This too wasn't entirely true, but I didn't have the time to explain.

I paused arranging my books. If these interruptions were going to carry on, then I couldn't work here. I'd get nothing done.

'It's more of a *study* holiday,' I said, hoping they'd take the hint.

'Ah. In which case, don't let us disturb you.'

'Though you know you're disturbing her just by saying that.'

'Well, at least I'm not arguing about it and disturbing her even more.'

They clearly weren't going to shut up. I was going to have to engage them in more conversation.

'Are you both staying here?' This was a pretty dumb question to ask. Of course they were staying here. Why else would they be here? They hardly looked like they'd broken in to sit by this fireplace.

'That's right,' said the first woman. 'I'm Marjorie and this is my sister, Marian.'

'I'm quite capable of saying my own name, thank you very much,' said Marian.

'I never said you weren't.'

'Is this the first time you've stayed here?' I asked, hoping to change the subject.

Both women cackled. 'No, we've been coming for years. Can't keep us away,' said Marian.

'That's right. We're the regulars,' said Marjorie.

My hands hovered over my books. Should I get more out, or start putting them away?

'Really? What's so good about here?'

'The sea air,' said Marjorie.

'The food,' said Marian.

They glared at each other again. I sneaked a look at the clock. It was half past seven. Breakfast was in half an hour and I'd done nothing.

I started putting my books back. I'd have to return to our room. There was no chance of getting anything done with this pair here.

'Well, it was nice to meet you.' I hitched my bag up and hurried into the corridor.

'See what you did?' said one of them. 'You scared her off. She was trying to do some work.'

'More like you did,' said the other. 'You're always bickering. Bound to make her feel uncomfortable. Why don't you ever learn to keep your mouth shut?'

I ran back to our room. Hattie was sitting up in bed now, checking her phone.

'Where did you go?' she asked.

'Bookroom,' I muttered. 'Only there were other people in there.'

'What people?'

'Two sisters – Marjorie and Marian.'

Hattie laughed. 'They were here when I last came. I'm surprised they're not dead, they were that old then.'

'Who are they?'

'They're twins, totally inseparable. Been coming every Easter since forever.'

Totally inseparable — that gave me the shivers. Imagine spending all your time with someone. And judging from the way they spoke to each other, a break from each other wouldn't be a bad thing.

'I wonder if there are any other guests I'll know,' said Hattie. 'I had no idea who that man was yesterday.'

'How many people can stay here?'

Hattie thought for a moment. 'Not sure exactly, but it's quite a few. Though it's only ever fully booked in the summer. Didn't Auntie Sadie say there were only four others staying this week?'

I unpacked my snack bag and put all the little bags containing my daily snacks in a row in one of the drawers. Getting that sorted made me feel calmer.

'Hope you've got enough for everyone,' said Hattie, looking over at my drawer.

'It was supposed to be your job, remember?' I said. 'Besides, how could I? You didn't tell me what your daily snacks are.'

'Did you ask?'

'Question twenty-three on the questionnaire.'

Hattie gave me a funny look before disappearing into the bathroom. People are weird sometimes.

CHAPTER 11

Hattie

Agnes had been fretting at the door for a clear five minutes.

'Breakfast is at eight,' she said, checking her watch for like the billionth time.

'It's eight-ish,' I said. Everything is 'ish' with Auntie Sadie — nothing is with Agnes. She huffed and folded her arms. I pulled a jumper on because, despite it being allegedly spring, it felt chilly.

'Ready,' I said, grinning at Agnes.

'Finally.'

We walked along the hall, through reception and into the dining room. It hadn't changed a bit since last year. Same square tables, same Seventies chairs, same chintz-fest. I loved it.

Marjorie and Marian were already seated at a

table in the window. There were a couple of other people in the dining room. Our table was right in the middle. No sign of Jake yet.

'Should we go and get him?' asked Agnes.

'He'll be down soon, I'm sure. Look, I'm starving. Let's just eat.'

Agnes must have been hungry too, as she agreed. Given the smell of bacon and coffee wafting out of the kitchen, she would have had to be super-human to resist.

'Good morning, chicks,' said Auntie Sadie, appearing from the kitchen. 'You sleep OK?'

'Yes, very well, thank you,' said Agnes.

'Yeah, lush, thanks,' I said.

'No Jake yet?'

'Nah, but he'll be down soon, I reckon,' I said.

'Are you going to wait for him?'

Agnes looked genuinely torn. Better help her out.

'Nope,' I said. 'We're here on time...'

'Ish,' muttered Agnes, clearly still sore about my timekeeping.

Auntie Sadie smiled. 'Great. Let me know what you want for your cooked breakfast, then help yourself to cereal and croissants and things over there.'

Did I say that I loved it here? This place was

amazing, especially now that I didn't have to share it with my wart of a brother. And the breakfast was just wow. I arranged my breakfast on the table, adjusted the cup of coffee and snapped a photo. Instagram lurves a breakfast shot.

We were getting stuck into the pastries, when Jake appeared in the doorway, rubbing his eyes.

'Decided you'd turn up?' said Agnes.

Jake grinned. 'The smell woke me.'

'Let Auntie Sadie know what you want for your cooked,' I told him. 'She's in the kitchen.'

He walked over to the doorway and I heard Auntie Sadie greet him like a long-lost son.

'Perhaps we should have asked him about his timekeeping,' said Agnes, as she spooned Rice Krispies into a bowl.

'Chill,' I said. 'We're on holiday. And besides, he's not that late.'

Agnes gave me a look, then poured her milk.

I forgot. There are no gradients with Agnes. He was either on time or late, there was no in-between.

'What shall we do today?' I asked, between mouthfuls, once Jake had sat down with a plate piled high with pastries.

Agnes rummaged in her pocket and got out a small notepad. 'I thought a couple hours of study, a bit of free time, then a few more hours of study this afternoon. Depending on how it goes, there's a chance we could have the evening off.'

Jake looked like I felt. 'You're not serious?' he said.

'Absolutely,' said Agnes, her face backing her up.

'Right. Well, I'm up for *a bit* of studying, but maybe starting tomorrow.'

It was Agnes' turn to look shocked. 'But…' she started.

I interrupted. I needed to get some photos and studying wasn't going to give me them. 'Listen, how about … you can study, and me and Jake can go sightseeing. Then we can meet up later. If your revision's gone well, we could go out somewhere this evening together. How does that sound?'

Agnes looked like she was making a mental pros and cons list.

'OK,' she said finally. 'What time shall we rendezvous?'

She had her pencil poised over her notepad. I had no idea what time.

'What would suit you best?'

She muttered to herself, while noting things down. 'Tea's at six, isn't it?'

I nodded.

'Let's meet at five-thirty. Then there's time for you to be late.'

I grinned. That seemed fair.

Auntie Sadie came in, carrying three plates piled with sausages, bacon, grilled tomatoes, beans and fried bread. Jake whooped.

'That looks legendary,' he said. Auntie Sadie grinned. Don't reckon many of her guests whoop when she serves them breakfast.

'I'll just introduce you to everyone, seeing as you're staying for the week,' she said. 'First, over here are Marjorie and Marian.'

'We've met,' said Agnes, nodding in their direction.

'Nice to see you again,' I said, smiling.

Marjorie and Marian did the obligatory 'My, haven't you grown' and 'What a young lady you've turned into' comments everyone feels compelled to say if they haven't seen you for more than a week.

Jake finished off a mouthful of beans. 'You look ever so similar. Are you sisters?'

'Twins,' said Marjorie, who was nearest me.

'Identical,' said Marian.

'How do people tell you apart?'

'Marjorie is the one with a vile temper,' snapped Marian.

'That's a bit rich,' said Marjorie.

'And over here,' said Auntie Sadie, deflecting, 'are another two of my regulars: Parveen Kapoor and Mr Giles Fitzgerald.'

Mr Fitzgerald nodded smartly in our direction.

Parveen smiled. 'Sadie, are you going to tell us who these delightful young people are?'

'This is my niece, Hattie, and her friends, Agnes and Jake. They're here for a study break.'

Parveen roared with laughter. 'A study break? Wow. Well, don't do too much studying. There's a world to explore out there. You don't want to miss out.'

Agnes bristled. 'We're exploring the world *by* studying.'

Parveen stopped laughing and looked at Agnes. 'You're right. Both are important.'

'Don't mind Parveen,' said Mr Fitzgerald. 'She gets excited when she thinks she can live vicariously through someone else.'

Parveen playfully hit his arm.

I must have looked confused, because Agnes hissed, 'It means she imagines she shares the fun you have.'

That's weird. Why would she think a study break was fun?

Once we'd finished breakfast, Jake said he needed to do something in his room so we arranged to meet up in half an hour. I went back to my room with Agnes. She set up her revision stuff at the desk and I sat on my bed.

I scrolled on my phone. Zara, Chelsea and Scarlett had been at a sleepover last night. The pit of my stomach knotted. There were pictures of face masks, nail varnish, DVDs and pizza. I wished I'd been there with them. I looked up to see Agnes hunched over her books, muttering about irregular verbs.

I found our group chat.

Why are you still doing this to me? I told you what happened. Can't we just be friends again?

It was sent before I had time to second-guess myself. I missed them. Totally. Like a part of me was lost.

I watched as it was read by each of them.

Chelsea left the group chat.

Then Zara, then Scarlett.

I stared at the screen. What had I done? How could I have been so stupid? Talk about inviting people to stomp on your heart. If I was ever in any doubt about how they felt about me this was a massive sign, neon-lit and flashing. Just in case I hadn't known. This may blow over as far as everyone else was concerned, but my friends were never going to let me back in.

I threw my phone onto my pillow and leaned my head back against the wall. My head hurt. Why couldn't they just listen? Why didn't they believe me?

Agnes was too busy with her French to notice the tears dripping off my chin.

CHAPTER 12

I'd hardly slept all night, which is why I'd nearly missed breakfast. My head had been pounding and seemed bursting full of every fear and question and what if. I had to make it stop. I had to try and find some calm. What if writing it down helped? I'd heard that once. Write all your thoughts down. But where to start?

Worst-case scenario

It's some sort of cancer. It's spread. It's everywhere. The doctor looks grave. My mum cries.

I stopped writing. I'm not sure that type of writing was helping. What about the opposite.

Best-case scenario

It's nothing horrible at all. A cyst. It clears up on its own. Or I go to the doctor and he says it's nothing and I'm embarrassed.

Embarrassment. That's my best-case scenario. To be fair, if it stopped my head from galloping along at a million miles an hour, I'd take it. I played it out in my head.

'Jake. Jake!' There was knocking at the door. I blinked. How long had I been staring out of the window for?

'Look, Jake, are you even in there?'

It was Hattie and she sounded ticked off.

'Hang on!'

I opened the door. Hattie was outside, holding her coat and wearing an expression.

'Sorry,' I said. 'Forgot the time.'

Hattie rolled her eyes. 'I need to get out. Agnes is doing my head in. All that revision can't be good for you.'

'You mean she's making you feel guilty about not doing any?'

I could see she was trying not to smile.

'Let me grab a hoodie.' I let the door go and Hattie caught it with her foot.

'Where do you fancy going?' she asked.

'No idea. I've never been to Weston before, so I've no clue what's here.'

Hattie thought for a moment. 'I reckon a walk along the front to the Grand Pier is the first thing you've got to experience. It's quintessentially Weston.'

'Fancy word!'

'I've been around Agnes too long.'

I laughed.

'Come on, then.' She pulled my arm. I let her. It was actually quite nice not to have to make the effort myself to get moving. I grabbed my hoodie and we left the room, the door banging shut behind us.

Hattie was down the stairs two at a time. 'And, after the pier, we could walk further on down the prom to Uphill. That's right at the far end. You get a really good view of Brean Down, and...'

This was going to be really good for me. I just had to stay in the moment and not let my thoughts wander off into thinking about... Stop it! You're doing it already. Concentrate. Concentrate on Hattie and what she's saying.

We walked down the road, the low wall of grey stone higgledy-piggledy next to us. As we reached the wide junction at the end of the road, we crossed to the prom, and instead of going right towards the Old Pier, we turned left. It was weird to see what had been an ordinary, close-packed street of houses fall away to stretched-out beach and sea and sky and along the horizon a squiggle of a distant shoreline.

'Wow,' I said. Or I would have if my words hadn't been blown out of my mouth by a gust of wind. My short hair was all on end and I felt it being whipped around. I could taste the salt in the air.

The sea was closer – much closer than it had been last night – and I could see the waves crashing on the mudflats just past the headland.

'Come on,' said Hattie. She seemed to be energised by the wind, her steps bouncier and her voice louder and smile wider. 'Isn't it just brilliant?'

She stopped to take a selfie. 'Come on, squeeze in.' She took several shots before uploading one.

The sun was out and the wind was up. This was good. My head was clearing. I didn't know if it was because of the writing or being out but I didn't care. Something was buzzing in my blood. I picked up my pace to catch up with Hattie, who was practically skipping down the pavement. The wide promenade ran along the top of the high sea wall, the sand a good twenty feet or so below us.

We stopped to look out towards the sea. The top of the wall was worn away, with dimples and holes in the stone, as if it had been made of sand washed away by the sea.

'This is the Marine Lake,' explained Hattie. 'There's a big wall that holds some of the sea back so there's always somewhere to paddle. The sea comes over the wall at high tide and when it goes out, all this water stays behind. There's even a walkway along the top of it. Brilliant, isn't it?'

I nodded. There were some little kids down on the sand, shrieking and jumping the tiny waves.

'So you can walk across the sea wall?'

'Of course! Not when the sea's right in; even the posts along it disappear underwater then. But it's loads of fun crossing just as the tide gets to it!'

I grinned.

'Let me get a picture of it,' said Hattie. She took several, and I watched as she put them on Instagram.

'OK, pier next,' said Hattie.

She walked along the promenade, talking almost non-stop and only ever standing on the dark grey stones, rather than the light grey or speckled ones. At first I didn't realise what she was doing, but once I did, it was tricky not to do the same.

'Have you always come on holiday to Weston? Cos your aunt's here?'

Hattie nodded. 'Yeah. She's had that bed and breakfast for years. Every February half-term she shuts it and has the whole family come and stay. It was brilliant when I was little. Everyone together, and a beach just on the doorstep. I loved it. Always flippin' freezing though.'

'And now?'

'Well, now it means I don't get to hang out with my friends.'

I thought a minute. 'So why are you here this week? I know you sit next to Agnes on the bus and everything, but she's not part of your group, is she?' I was sure I'd seen her hanging out with a group of girls. Quite a scary group too.

Hattie stopped. I had to walk back to her. Her face was flushed and she was blinking a lot.

'They're busy this week. That's all.'

She started walking again, but she was no longer playing the 'only grey stones' game and all her bounce had gone.

There was something not right, but I couldn't figure out what. And I didn't want to put my foot in it.

'Well, that's lucky for me and Agnes.' I smiled.

'Ha!' she said. 'So? What about your friends?'

My friends. Well, more like my team. I'd always been part of the basketball team. Until two weeks ago. When it all seemed suddenly irrelevant. I pushed the thought back down again.

'Yeah, I used to be part of the basketball team, but … I'm not anymore.'

'How come? Get kicked off?'

'No. I told them I had to concentrate on my exams.' Not exactly a lie. It's what I'd let them believe.

'That go down well, did it?'

She saw right through me.

'Not particularly.'

I'd not told anyone. I'd not even told my mum that I'd come off the team. She didn't need to know. I'd be leaving the school in a couple of months anyway, so why make her worry?

'So you're not too flush on the friends' front either?'

'You could say that.'

We walked together for a moment or two in silence.

'So…' I said, reckoning a change of mood would be good. 'This pier. Is it better than the old one?'

Immediately, Hattie was back to chatting and laughing, but I was left wondering what was going on with Hattie that she wasn't telling me. And had she realised I was hiding something too?

CHAPTER 13

Once Hattie and Jake had left, I revised while keeping an eye on the time. I stopped only for lunch. At three exactly, I packed away my revision notes and pulled on my shoes and coat. I had the address for Rose, and I was going to see her. I could feel the excitement fizzing inside me.

It took me about twenty minutes to walk there. Number thirty-three. I stopped outside and double-checked I had the correct address. I had. Rose would be pleased to see me, I was sure of that.

I rang the bell and waited. A tall girl answered the door. 'Yes?'

'Is Rose in?'

'No. Sorry. She moved out yesterday.'

'Moved out?' Why would she move out?

'Yeah. She's renting her own place.'

I needed to know where. I needed to see her and it needed to be today.

'What's her new address?'

The girl pulled a face. 'I'm not sure. Somewhere close to the centre, because she's pleased she can still walk to work.'

How could she not know where Rose had moved to?

I walked away down the path. What could I do now? Could I text Rose and ask her? She might not be pleased I'd ignored what she'd said. It would be different if I was actually in front of her. What about Mum? I bet Mum would know. Rose always tells her everything. But Mum thought I was in Blackpool. I checked the time and Hattie's Instagram. It looked like they were on their way home, though, oddly, there was no mention of Jake. Anyway, I needed to be back before Hattie and Jake, so I started the walk back to the bed and breakfast. It seemed further going back. Perhaps that's what excitement does for you.

I heard them before I saw them: Hattie shrieking with laughter and Jake laughing too. The door to my room burst open and the noise got louder.

'Ah, Agnes!' said Hattie. 'How was your day? We've had the best time. You should have come with us.'

'Why should I?' I don't like the word should. It makes me itchy.

'Because we went on the pier – they have some crazy rides – and then we had hot dogs and I got this hat, and…' The hat was a garish pink with 'I ♥ Weston' on the front.

Jake was smiling.

'Weren't you tempted to get a hat?' I asked, interrupting Hattie.

'Nah, not my style,' he said. I'll be honest. I'm not sure it's many people's style.

'What have you been doing?' asked Hattie. She seemed annoyed with me, though I had no idea why.

'Revising. History. I've got a list of dates and laws all ready to memorise and I've filed and colour-coded my notes.'

'Sounds riveting.'

'It has been.'

If they'd been interested, if they'd been paying attention, they'd have clocked that this wouldn't have taken all day. But there was no point in telling Hattie and Jake. It would only lead to questions and explanations I didn't want to give.

'A solid day's work,' I said, to reinforce the idea that I hadn't moved from the spot all day.

'In which case,' said Jake, 'you'll be wanting a break from revision this evening. We're going out. All three of us.'

'But...'

'It is at least partly a holiday,' he said.

'And you do have to have breaks.' Hattie seemed to be back to her normal self again.

I looked from one to the other. I couldn't say I wanted to do more work, having supposedly been working all day.

'I'm not going anywhere noisy. I hate noisy places.'

'Fair enough,' said Jake, grinning. 'The pier was loud enough for me.'

Hattie laughed. 'I had to keep repeating myself because he couldn't hear what I was saying.'

'Sounds horrific,' I said.

They both laughed. Why was that funny? Noise so loud you can't hear what people are saying is awful.

'Quiet night out it is,' said Hattie. 'I think I can just about cope.'

We left straight after Auntie Sadie's amazing evening meal. Rich cottage pie and heaps of vegetables with the most amazing gravy I'd ever tasted. Jam sponge and custard for pudding. I felt so full.

The evenings were getting lighter and the sky still had a pinky glow as we walked along the promenade. The wind had dropped since earlier, but the temperature had stayed warm. For the first day this year, it felt like summer. Only you still needed a jumper.

All along the front were bars and restaurants with long frontages: tables and chairs crammed into every available space. Not many of them were filled. I guessed it was still early in the season. At least wherever we ended up wouldn't be really crowded. Seagulls soared above us, cawing and cackling, and loops of lights between the lamp posts swung gently, giving a feeling that we weren't quite on solid ground.

We walked further on, past the pier and up into the town. It was slightly busier there, with shops among the bars, though most of them were closed.

'Let's get a drink somewhere,' said Hattie.

Jake spotted a burger place on the corner. We ordered three chocolate milkshakes and sat in the corner window, slurping through the straws. The lights were bright neon against the dark blue twilight outside.

Hattie had her phone out and was alternating between scrolling and tapping, with every now and then a frantic burst of typing with both thumbs.

Jake stared out of the window. The kind of stare where you don't really look at anything in particular. Like he was miles away and he'd left his eyes resting on something.

I looked out of the window too. Hattie clearly was lost in her social-media world. And I'm not one to start an unnecessary conversation. Companionable silence is a skill we've lost as human beings, I reckon.

I was debating this in my head, when I saw her. Rose. Hurrying along the pavement opposite. She'd got her head down and a bag over her shoulder, walking fast. It looked like she was carrying some takeaway pizzas. She must be going home. Quick! This was my opportunity. I had to follow her.

I jumped up, leaving my milkshake on the table.

'Where you going?' called Hattie. *Now* she'd decided to pay attention to the world around her? Just my luck.

I pushed open the heavy doors, and ran into the big square. Where had Rose gone? I looked frantically round, searching in every direction. She can't have just vanished.

But she had. There were a few people strolling across the square but Rose wasn't one of them. I checked again.

'Are you OK?'

Hattie had followed me out, her phone still in her hand.

'Of course.'

'What did you run out for?'

'I ... um ... thought I saw ... something,' I said. I'm a horrible liar.

Jake was watching us both through the window.

'I just ... I ... um ...'

Rose had gone. I had had my chance. I should have been quicker.

'Cramp,' I said, rubbing my calf and hobbling back inside. 'Needed to stretch it out.'

Hattie shot me a funny look. When I got back inside, Jake smiled.

'Everything OK?'

I didn't answer. Everything was not OK.

What was I doing here? It's so odd. With Jake, a boy I hardly knew, and Hattie, my acquaintance from the bus? I should have found the money and come on my own, because then I wouldn't be here, wasting time, when I could be either revising or looking for Rose. I bit the end of my straw flat. No point wishing that now. I was stuck with them.

At least now I'd seen Rose. My heart was thudding in my chest, the thrill of seeing her filling my body with happiness. Tomorrow would be my chance to see her again. She'd definitely be at work, so I would find her there.

CHAPTER 14

Hattie

My phone was going off on one after breakfast on Monday morning. There barely seemed to be a break between the tiny buzzes coming from the table by my bed. It was chucking it down outside, so we'd taken ages with breakfast, eating slice after slice of toast and drinking mug after mug of Auntie Sadie's gorgeous hot chocolate. But breakfast couldn't last forever and Agnes had already set up her revision camp in the bookroom, telling the other residents that they would be welcome if they were quiet. She'd added that she didn't think this was unreasonable, for what was essentially a library. Marjorie and Marian had totally met their match.

I picked up my phone. I'd been tagged into a conversation. It looked like there were almost all of my English group in the chat. I could see Zara's name coming up, then Chelsea's. Scarlett's not in my English set.

So, is it true?

I've heard it is

Who said?

People

I was about to leave the group, when I stopped.

So Hattie really did it then

Totally

My hands started to shake a bit, but I kept hold of my phone and watched as the messages kept coming. They were from Sharleen. She sits three rows back from me, and she was the one who was utterly convinced I'd done it. I had the creeping feeling things weren't dying down. It didn't seem like anyone had noticed I was in the group. Or maybe they knew and didn't care.

Doesn't surprise me.

Me neither. She's always been like that.

Yeah. Real two-faced. Says one thing to your face, then another thing behind your back.

Can't trust her

I could feel the knot of panic growing in me. The world blurred, the only thing in focus, this conversation. They had to be talking about the party.

Sorry, late to the conversation. What have I missed?

We're just talking about Hattie and Bailey at the party the other week.

I felt sick. I'd known people were talking about me, but that was theoretical 'people'. This conversation was real people. People I knew.

A lad in another form had put on a party. A pre-GCSE party. His parents had made the mistake of going away for a weekend and leaving him home alone. Probably started out as a few of his mates but ended up being pretty much the whole of year eleven, apart from a few, like Agnes, who aren't big into parties.

Oh, I heard about that. She kissed him I'd heard

Yeah, Scarlett's pretty upset

I bet. She's supposed to be her mate

Some mate

Yeah. Who needs friends like that?

It had been dark, and there was loud music blaring out of a stereo in the doorway to the kitchen, so I'd gone into the garden. Kids were everywhere, all up the stairs, in the hall, I even spotted a couple who had taken up residence in the hall cupboard in a nest of coats, but the garden was quieter, and I'd lost the others and thought they could be out there.

I'd walked round the garden, checking right up

at the top by the vegetable plot, and in a small cutesy summer house and round the patio. I was just having a final look round the side of the house before I went back inside when Bailey found me.

'You seen the others?' I asked.

'They're all inside, I think. I just got a bit sick of the noise, so I've come outside.'

'Yeah, me too.'

'Fancy finding a bench? I've got a bowl of crisps, and I reckon I'll be sick if I eat them all myself.'

'Don't eat them all then,' I said, laughing.

'Can't help myself,' he said, laughing too.

We found a bench, tucked in by a large hedge and an overgrown flowerbed. We chatted and laughed for ages. Then I started to feel really cold.

'I reckon I'm going to head in, I'm freezing.'

I went to stand up but Bailey held on to my hand. I should have known then. Why didn't I know? Why hadn't I realised?

'It's been really great this evening. I love talking to you.'

'Yeah, it's been nice,' I said.

And that's when he did it. He kissed me. Right on the lips.

I must have frozen for a second, the shock paralysing me. And then I pulled away.

'What did you do that for?'

'I thought that's what you wanted? You've spent the whole evening with me. You've been flirting with me.'

'I haven't. And, besides, you're Scarlett's boyfriend. I wouldn't be flirty with my mate's boyfriend.'

'And yet, here we are.'

I could hear his grin in the dark.

Sharleen said she was chewing his face off

I'd heard it was in the garden

Yeah

I felt sick. I hadn't kissed him, he'd kissed me. But Scarlett. Scarlett hadn't believed me.

No wonder she's not been hanging out with them

Yeah, who wants someone like that around?

I started typing, my fingers shaking, my heart pounding. I couldn't sit here and do nothing.

Sharleen lied. That isn't what happened. Why does everyone just presume all the time?

You have been blocked.

I'd run away. Run away from Bailey and back into the brightly lit kitchen which was full of people laughing, singing and dancing in what little space there was. I had to find the others. I could taste the crisps we'd been sharing. I grabbed a coke and swigged a mouthful. Ugh. I spat into the kitchen sink. I had to find them. I wouldn't say anything, but I'd be safe with them. Bailey would be mad to say anything.

Then I saw them through the doorway, sat in the lounge, all of them squashed up together on a sofa. How had I not seen them earlier? I pushed people out of the way to get to them. It would be so good just to forget this ever happened.

'Hey!' I said, raising my voice slightly so I could be heard over the music.

Scarlett turned her head away.

'What are you doing here?' said Chelsea.

I didn't think I'd heard her right.

'What?'

'Think you can snog someone else's boyfriend and pretend like nothing's happened?'

The words echoed around my head. How did they know?

'I didn't,' I said. 'I didn't kiss him.'

'You know who we're talking about then?' Scarlett stood up. She took a step towards me. 'That's a bit weird, don't you think, if *nothing's* happened.'

'That's not what I said. I didn't kiss him.' I took a deep breath, knowing that the next sentence would destroy her. 'He kissed me.'

'That's not what Sharleen saw,' said Zara. 'She said she saw you kissing Bailey.'

What?

'She's lying.'

'That's pretty harsh,' said Scarlett. 'Why would Sharleen lie? She's seeming like a very good friend at the moment.'

'But that isn't what happened.' I wanted to scream it so she would listen. Would believe me. Would make everything go back to normal. 'You've got to believe me. I wouldn't do that to you.'

'Don't believe her,' said Zara. 'That's exactly what she would say.'

'I don't think you should stay here, do you?' said Chelsea, putting her arm around Scarlett's shoulders.

And I hadn't stayed. I'd run from the house, run all the way home. They'd not spoken to me since.

Everything felt so wrong. Why was I even in Weston? Stuck here with Jake and Agnes? I wanted my friends back so badly it hurt. The friends who'd known me for years, who understood me, who got me. But, then again, maybe they didn't. I stared out of the window as the rain drummed on it, streaming down and blurring the view. My heart was breaking and I didn't know how to stop it.

CHAPTER 15

This was exactly the reason I hadn't wanted to stay at home. Coming here was supposed to help. Stop me thinking. Well, that plan had been a colossal failure because here I was, utterly obsessing about everything.

Breakfast had been good. It was only since then that I'd been drowning in thoughts. We'd eaten loads and Hattie and me stayed on to eat more toast after Agnes had gone to revise.

But Hattie had disappeared into her room and I hadn't seen her in ages. The rain was not helping. It always makes me feel worse, even when there's nothing really to feel bad about. Not like this.

I knew I really should tell someone. Probably a doctor, maybe Mum. I always got that far, before my brain ran off screaming. There was no way I could tell my mum. What if she wanted to look? The cringe overwhelmed me. She always puts on this funny voice whenever she's talking about anything like that. Like it's important I understand all the facts, so she delivers them, formally, like a teacher. Must be weird for her too. There should be some parenting DVD with all the gross and embarrassing and weird stuff parents have to tell their kids; then they could just give the latest version to their kids at each birthday. Save everyone the cringefest.

What if I didn't tell my mum? Told my stepdad? He'd always been pretty cool about everything. Perhaps he'd tell me it was all fine, and not to worry, it was normal. What was normal? Perhaps it had always been there and I'd just never noticed. Perhaps everyone had it? I'd get to the doctor's and he'd laugh at me for my lack of anatomical knowledge.

It shouldn't be like this. I should be confident with my body, unashamed about asking questions. So many shoulds, and the one important should, *what should I do*, was completely without an answer.

I could google it. Find out some options. But the thought terrified me. What if the news wasn't good? What if it was really, really not good? Worst-case scenarios piled in as usual: bald heads, crying friends and my mum... I blocked them off. The lump wasn't any problem; it didn't really hurt. But the headaches and now the stomach pains were worrying. It was all this sitting around thinking that was no good for me.

I picked up my phone and checked Hattie's Instagram. Lots of pictures of breakfast, of the hot chocolates and toast, but still no mention of me or Agnes. I kind of get it. We're not in her circle of friends. But still. It felt a bit weird.

I got off my bed and went to look for Hattie. That was why I was here – to keep her company when Agnes was buried in books. I knocked on her door. I knew Agnes would be in the bookroom and that I wasn't to disturb. There was no chance Hattie had gone out in this rain.

'Yeah?' said Hattie, from the other side of the door.

'It's me, can I come in?'

'Sure.'

The door swung open and Hattie disappeared back into the room, leaving me to catch the door as it shut.

'So,' I said, trying to cheer myself out of my grump. 'What's the plan today?'

'I don't know, Jake, it's raining, so most things are off. How about you come up with something?'

'Are you OK?'

'Totally. Why wouldn't I be?'

'Well, you just seem, I don't know, a bit…' I wanted to say angry, but didn't actually want her to direct it my way.

'A bit what, Jake?'

'Upset.'

Her face wobbled, but she quickly covered it up. 'Well, I'm not.'

'Oh. Good, then.'

'Look, I was just in the middle of some … revision, so if you don't mind…?'

'Oh, of course, sorry to disturb. See you at lunch?'

'Yes, lunch.'

She escorted me to the door and shut it behind me. Weird. Revision, yet there wasn't a single textbook, notebook or marker pen out. Just a scrumpled-up duvet and her phone. But she clearly had something going on, and I wasn't going to push it.

I walked along the corridor into the lounge. Auntie Sadie had lit the fire, and although the day wasn't super-chilly, it did warm the room nicely.

Marjorie and Marian both looked as if they were asleep in the armchairs and Mr Fitzgerald and Parveen were playing a game of chess. Bramble was lying spread out under their table. Mr Fitzgerald beckoned me over.

'Come and give me a hand, lad. I could do with a young brain on my side. She's properly beating me.'

I walked over and looked at the board. He wasn't wrong. Parveen's pieces looked to be in a textbook formation, ready to pounce.

Parveen was smiling a little half-smile, obviously enjoying the impending doom she was about to wreak on Mr Fitzgerald.

I sucked my teeth.

'It's bad, isn't it?' said Mr Fitzgerald. I nodded and grinned. Parveen smiled even more.

'You could always surrender graciously,' she said. 'If you don't think you can win.'

'Oh, it's always worth trying. You never know when you might find a way to defend yourself.'

'OK then. Fighting talk,' said Parveen, rubbing her hands together. 'Pull up a chair, Jake, and I'll show you how to deconstruct an army.'

Mr Fitzgerald chuckled.

In fifteen moves, Mr Fitzgerald's king was cornered, his army lying helpless along the side of the board.

'Obviously, I let her win,' Mr Fitzgerald said to me.

'Poppycock,' said Parveen, 'you're as competitive as I am. You were trying to win right up to the end.'

Mr Fitzgerald laughed again. 'She's got the measure of me.'

Parveen held out her hand. 'Always a pleasure to beat you, Giles.'

Mr Fitzgerald shook her hand. 'Likewise.'

'OK, Jake, why don't you take my place? I'm going to find my book.' Parveen got up and patted my shoulder before leaving the room.

'So, lad? Fancy a game?'

'Sure.' I moved to Parveen's seat and started setting up the pieces, ready to play. The first few moves were standard, mainly clearing the pawns to let the other pieces do their jobs.

'So, then,' said Mr Fitzgerald, 'exams in a few weeks, is it?'

'Yeah. Though I keep forgetting.'

Mr Fitzgerald's eyebrows shot up, though he didn't say anything.

'I seem to have lots of other things on my mind.'

'Girls?' asked Mr Fitzgerald.

I laughed. 'I wish.'

Mr Fitzgerald gave his deep chuckle.

I looked at him. He looked old, maybe he was wise too.

'I've got a … friend. He's got something going on.'

Mr Fitzgerald tipped his head to one side, inviting me to go on.

'He can either ignore it and hope it goes away, or he has to tell people. And, well, that isn't all that … comfortable.'

I could feel the heat rising through my cheeks. He would think I was mad. Talking in riddles.

Mr Fitzgerald studied the board for a moment or two, stroking his moustache.

'I've always found,' he started slowly, 'that knowledge isn't something to be feared. Knowledge brings you power, options and opportunities. I don't know what it is that's worrying your friend, and I'm not going to ask. But I've rarely found ignoring a problem helps.'

He moved his knight. 'Check.'

My king was cornered.

CHAPTER 16

I know statistically speaking it's more likely to rain at the coast than inland, but the reality of this really sucked.

It had been thirty-six hours. Thirty-six hours of the same people, the same air, the same everything. Thirty-six hours of not being able to sneak out to see Rose. Hattie's Auntie Sadie was the only one who saw any kind of upside to the weather. She's been dogmatically cheerful and even that was starting to annoy me.

'It's due to stop raining mid-morning,' she said over breakfast. 'Why don't you go out somewhere? It'll do you good to get some air in your lungs.'

I wanted to point out that we'd got air in our lungs. Else we'd not be here. But I didn't. Reckon

Mum would have been proud of me. I got a literal groove in my tongue from biting on it so hard.

'Sounds great,' said Hattie. She was busy taking pictures of her breakfast again. She looked tired. I'm not too good on subtle stuff, but even I could see the dark circles under her eyes.

'Good plan,' said Jake. He didn't look too much better.

The instant I could, I was going to head out to find Rose. Hattie and Jake could do what they liked. I had my own plans.

By mid-morning, the rain had dried up, the clouds had cleared and weak sunshine was doing its best to push through the net curtains. I sneaked a look over my physics notes. Then I stretched and closed my book. This needed to seem like no big deal. They mustn't come with me.

Hattie was sprawled on her bed. She'd spent pretty much the entire day there yesterday, leaning on a propped-up pillow, her phone on permanent charge.

I picked up my coat, pulled it on and tucked my phone into my pocket.

'Where are you going?' said Hattie, barely looking up.

'Nowhere. Just need some air.'

Hattie stretched. 'That actually sounds like a good idea. I'll come too.'

What? No. This was not the plan. How would I get to the council offices to find Rose with Hattie there?

'It's going to be really boring,' I said. 'So dull.'

Hattie frowned a bit.

Jake was lying on the floor near the window. 'You know, getting out is a good idea. Give me a minute, I'll grab my hoodie.' He opened the door. 'See you in the entrance in five?' Then he left.

'What's up?' said Hattie.

'Nothing.' I tried to laugh, but it came out wrong.

'Our company that bad, is it?' Hattie sounded strange.

'You could be worse,' I acknowledged by way of concession.

Hattie frowned.

I don't get her. She's spent her entire time on her phone. She can't expect to win a popularity contest with people she's basically ignored. And I'd checked out her Instagram – lots about how amazing Weston is. Still not a word or a picture about me or Jake.

How I wished I could go out on my own.

'Fine. I'll get my shoes,' said Hattie, sticking her phone in her pocket.

The pit of my stomach felt heavy.

Within five minutes we were outside. The air was fresh and cool. It had stopped raining but everywhere was still soaked as we walked towards the promenade, before turning left along the seafront.

Hattie had her phone again, and was completely out of the loop. Jake was quiet. Both were trailing along a few paces behind me. Every few minutes, Hattie stopped to take a photo or a selfie. At least this left me free to look out for Rose. Every person we passed, I checked. Every person on the opposite side of the road, I checked. None of them were her. As we got closer to the centre of Weston, there were more and more people. Obviously the break in the weather had brought them out, all of them sniffing the air.

This was pointless. I needed to get to the council offices. Rose would be at work, not wandering round the streets.

'Come on,' I said to the others.

Jake hurried up a little, but soon slowed down again. Hattie made no sign she'd even heard me. She stopped to take a photo of a seagull.

'Would you please just hurry up,' I snapped.

'Don't get your knickers in a twist,' muttered Hattie. 'What's the rush anyway?'

So she could hear me.

'Oh, nice of you to join us.'

Hattie looked up from her screen. 'What d'you mean by that?'

Jake glanced nervously at us both. We were still walking, past the pier, past the old Sea Life Centre and the disused lido and were now out by the miniature railway.

'You know,' I said, not even bothering to turn around.

'I'm here, aren't I? Not anywhere else.'

'You didn't have to come,' I snapped back. 'If you wanted to be on your phone, you could have stayed in.'

'That's really unfair. I'm not always on my phone. I'm right here with you. What more do you want?' Hattie's voice was raised.

'Really? You don't know what's wrong? You've been posting the whole week – amazing holiday, amazing time. But not one mention of me or Jake. Nothing.'

Jake was shifting about uncomfortably.

Hattie's face flushed red.

'Jake? That doesn't bother you, does it? I bet you've not even noticed.'

Jake shuffled his feet. 'Err, I had noticed actually. But that's fine. It's your account. You can do what you like.'

Someone was walking along the opposite pavement. I turned to see if it was Rose.

Hattie turned on me. 'What *are* you doing? You keep staring at people. What's wrong with you?'

That was it.

'There is NOTHING wrong with me. Nothing at all.'

'Well, what you're doing is hardly normal, is it?'

She looked towards Jake for confirmation. Jake didn't say anything.

'Well, it's not,' she said. 'There's something going on with you and I want to know what it is. Auntie Sadie says you've been going out on your own, when Jake and me aren't around. But you've told us you've been revising the whole time. Are you lying or is my aunt?'

'What? You're accusing me of lying to you?' I mean I had, but I wasn't ready to tell. And besides it was a lie of omission – low on the gradient of lying. 'That's outrageous. Why would I lie to you?'

'I don't know,' said Hattie, flinging her arms

open wide. 'You tell me. But I'm pretty sure my aunt wouldn't have made it up.'

'At least I haven't been on my phone 24/7. At least I've been present. Unlike you.'

Hattie's eyes narrowed. 'I've got stuff going on, OK? You wouldn't understand.'

'I understand perfectly. You'd rather be with your mates than hanging out with us, and the only way you can do that is by being online. Heaven forbid that anyone might actually know you're here with US.'

Jake stepped between us. 'Look. Let's not fight…'

'No one's fighting with you, Jake,' I said. 'But why don't you both admit it? You'd both prefer to be somewhere else. Because I know, I certainly would.'

Hattie gave a look, then turned on her heel and walked away down the beach.

Good riddance.

CHAPTER 17

Hattie

How dare she? I couldn't believe she'd said that. After everything I've done for her – sorting out somewhere for her to stay in Weston, listening to her go on and on about revision.

She makes me so mad. She's so SELFISH. All about her holiday and her revision and what she wants to do and what she wants me to do. Well, enough. No more. We can pack up and go home this afternoon. I don't want to stay here any longer than I have to with people like her. And I can put what I want on my Instagram. They don't understand what it's like.

I was walking fast across the beach. The tide was coming in, but was still in the distance. As I walked past a wooden sign I felt like punching it.

Agnes just makes me SO mad. Who does she think she is?

I could hear her shouting in the distance behind me, but I ignored her and sped up. Brean Down seemed a lot closer, only a short stretch of sand away. I turned towards it. I had to slow down a bit as the sand was getting wetter and stickier.

Agnes was still shouting and maybe Jake was, too. A deeper voice was calling something but I couldn't make out the words. I'd show them. There was no way I was turning around to go back to them. No way.

The voices were more distant now. They'd given up, obviously. Finally realised I wasn't going back. Good.

My foot made a loud squelching noise as I pulled it out of the sand. I laughed. That was a weird sound. The next step was the same. On, the third step, my foot didn't come out at all.

I couldn't move it. I pulled hard, but my left leg had sunk up to the ankle. My whole foot had disappeared under the sand. I couldn't see my trainer at all.

The sign I'd passed flashed through my mind, suddenly clear.

Sinking sand. Dangerous. Do not pass.

I tried to lift my right foot, but that had sunk into the sand too. Both feet were stuck.

I tried rocking, but that just made my legs go further in. The cold, wet sand gripped my ankles. I mustn't panic. Worse thing you can do. I know that much. Thing was, I didn't know what I *should* be doing.

I stood still and tried to think. Think. What are you supposed to do? I'm sure I know. Is it struggle? Or definitely don't struggle? It was kind of crucial to get it right.

I reached for my phone. No signal. Dammit.

My feet were quite far apart and it was hard to keep my balance. I'd have to concentrate on one foot at a time. Get one foot out, step back, then unstick the other one. I could do this. I mustn't panic. There must be no panicking.

I started to dig around my right foot, scrabbling out the wet sand with my fingers. Every handful I threw away was replaced almost immediately with more waterlogged sand. I moved faster, but it made me wobble. My arms shot out, trying to regain my balance. I looked at my feet again.

Instead of having loosened my feet, the sand was now even further up my legs, reaching mid-shin.

What now? I twisted around to see if I could find Agnes and Jake, but I couldn't see them anywhere. There were a few people right in the distance, walking along the prom, but I doubted they'd hear me if I shouted.

The sound of a wave breaking made me look back. The sea was loads closer now, only a few metres away. My stomach clenched. I knew the tide came in fast, but this was a rather brutal way to find out just how fast. Perhaps I would be above the tideline?

I checked to see if there was a line of seaweed nearby. Instead my eyes fell on the sign I'd walked past. The tideline on the pole was near the top. And the pole was taller than I was.

I glanced back at the sea. It was closer again. Crap, crap, crap. Perhaps now would be a good time to panic.

'Help! Help me! Someone, help me! I'm stuck. HELP!'

I waved my arms and felt my legs sink in further. The clammy grip of the sand was at my knees. '*HELP!*'

If I had something to use as a wedge, or something that I could lean on... Anything. I searched around me. Nothing. No bits of driftwood even. Just metre after metre of rippled sand.

A wave reached my foot and I felt the cold water numb my skin through the sand.

I shouted again. With every decibel I could muster.

I looked back towards the promenade. Agnes! Jake! They were both running towards me. Agnes was carrying something big but I couldn't quite make out what. I couldn't hear what they were shouting either, but the sight of them made me wave and yell even louder. I sank deeper, the waves now lapping around me every few seconds. I started to cry. Even if they got to me, how were they going to get me out? What if they got stuck too?

'Stop!' I shouted. 'Don't come any closer. It's sinking sand. You'll only get stuck too.'

They must have been close enough to hear me, because they both skidded to a stop.

'I'm stuck. Get help. But don't come any closer.'

They were talking. I couldn't hear what they were saying. Jake squeezed Agnes' arm and started running back across the beach. Where was he going? Please, please, was he going for help?

He waved his phone around above his head as he ran, trying to get signal.

Agnes walked towards me. Slowly. But she was definitely heading my way.

'Stop. Don't get stuck.'

'Don't worry. I know what I'm doing,' she shouted back.

Seriously? There was no way she knew what she was doing.

'No. You don't. Stop. You'll get stuck too. And the tide's coming in.'

'Stop waving your arms.'

I hadn't even noticed I was.

'You must not panic.'

'Easy for you to say. You're not stuck.'

Agnes stopped. She was only a few paces from me.

'It feels scary but you've got to stay still. At least until I'm with you.'

She'd brought a deckchair with her. She must have pinched it off the stack at the top of the ramp to the beach. Was she planning to relax while watching me drown?

'Just do exactly as I tell you.'

'Do you seriously know what you're doing?'

'Could you please stop thinking you know better than me, just this once? Of course I know what I'm doing. I wouldn't say it otherwise.'

I sniffed. 'OK. Sorry. Tell me. What do I need to do?'

'I've already said. Stay still. And take some deep breaths.'

'To calm me down?'

'No, it keeps you buoyant.'

I wish I hadn't asked. I sucked in a lungful of air.

Agnes picked her way closer. She took off her shoes and threw them back up the beach.

'Can you get your shoes off?'

I wriggled my feet.

'I don't think so. It's all pretty tight in the foot zone right now.'

'OK.' Agnes was now really close and her feet were starting to sink too. She didn't seem to notice. 'I want you to lie down.'

'You have got to be kidding me. That's closer to the water.'

'I'm going to lie the deckchair down flat on the sand. You lie on the frame. It reduces the pressure on your legs and feet. Then you gradually work them loose. And *voilà*. You're free.'

How did she keep so freakin' calm?

She crouched and pushed the deckchair, folded flat, towards me. 'Right. Lower yourself onto that.'

I hesitated.

'Do it.'

I awkwardly fell sideways, the wooden deckchair banging on the side of my hip.

'Right, now start trying to wriggle your feet out.'

The water was rising fast. My hair was wet and my left side was underwater.

I wiggled my feet as fast as I could. The pressure was lessening. With a slip and a suck, my right foot came free.

'And now the other.'

Agnes' voice was calm.

'I can't. It just won't come out.'

'It will. You can do it.'

I began to cry again. I felt so tired. A wave washed over my face and I sat up a bit. I didn't like to think it but I couldn't help it. This might be it.

A splash behind me and Agnes climbed onto the other side of the deckchair.

'What are you doing? You're going to get stuck too. There's no point us both … us both … erm … you know.'

'Drowning?'

Trust Agnes to say it.

'Yeah, drowning. Cheers, Agnes.' I laughed a hollow laugh.

'No one's going to drown.'

I didn't feel so sure.

She sat right behind me so I could sit up and lean on her.

'No one. Is going. To drown.'

CHAPTER 18

Jake

'Coastguard, please. And perhaps an ambulance too. Quickly.'

The idea of needing an ambulance made me sick. My hand was shaking. Actually, all of me was shaking. I held tight to my phone. I mustn't drop it.

I kept my eyes on Agnes and Hattie the whole time I was speaking to the 999 operator. Agnes had moved really close to Hattie and then had knelt down next to her. Hattie was lying at a funny angle and I think she'd managed to get one of her feet free. Now the other one, I hoped. Come on. I started repeating it over and over. Like a wish to the universe to step in and help.

'You're doing great,' said the operator. 'Stay on the line and tell me if anything changes.' In the far distance, I could hear sirens. What were they going to do when they got here? Perhaps they had special equipment to get to them. The waves were now much higher. Every time one broke, both Agnes and Hattie disappeared for a moment under the water. The helplessness was screaming through me.

'Stay on the roadside where you've got signal and so they can find you,' said the operator, like she could read my thoughts. An ambulance rounded the corner, lights flashing, and sirens blaring.

'I can see the ambulance,' I said into my phone and waved my arm wildly above my head. Hattie and Agnes surely didn't have long. The ambulance pulled up at the kerb and two paramedics jumped out.

'They're over there,' I said, pointing. They kept disappearing under the waves. We were too late. My heart was pounding. My vision blurred a bit. I was going to stand here and watch them die.

One of the paramedics patted me on the shoulder. 'Look,' she said. 'Coastguard are on their way.'

There was a buzz, distant at first, like a fly, then closer and louder. Swinging right out, a hovercraft flew across the beach from further along the prom, before hugging the waterline. Two fluorescent yellow-clad people were in it and they were heading straight for Agnes and Hattie.

I ran down the steps onto the beach, and stumbled across the sand as fast as I could. One of the yellow people was holding out a hand to Agnes, ready to pull her into the craft. It didn't look like she wanted to go. But after a few seconds, Agnes was unceremoniously hauled head-first into the hovercraft.

The crew turned their attention to Hattie.

For a tense few seconds they worked at pulling and prising at Hattie's leg, until at last she popped up. Then she too was pulled into the hovercraft. The paramedics joined me on the beach, stretcher and emergency bag with them. The hovercraft started moving towards us, its skirt blown up round it.

'Stand back, all right, kid?' said the paramedic who'd spoken to me before. 'Let us sort your friends out, OK?'

I nodded. I just wanted them to be all right.

The hovercraft came up the beach and stopped near to us. Hattie was swiftly lifted out onto the stretcher. A blanket was wrapped round her and the paramedics immediately started checking her over. Her eyes were shut. Her lips were blue.

Agnes climbed out and came to stand next to

me. She was shaking. I could hear her teeth chattering.

'You all right?'

'Bit chilly,' she said. Her face was pale. I wanted to hug her, but guessed that wouldn't be something she'd like.

'Here,' I said. I took off my jumper and handed it to her. 'But I want it back, all right?'

She took the jumper. 'Thanks.'

Silently, we went back to watching Hattie. Suddenly she coughed. They rolled her and she coughed up a ton of water. Then opened her eyes.

The universe had listened. She wasn't dead.

'Right,' said the other paramedic. 'Let's get her off the beach; that tide's going to be at us any minute. Thanks, guys.'

The hovercraft crew nodded, before buzzing back off down the beach the way they'd come.

'I've never been in a hovercraft before,' said Agnes, as we walked up the beach behind the two paramedics carrying Hattie.

'Bit of an extreme way to have a ride.' I couldn't get Hattie's face out of my head. That had been really close. I was feeling cold, too, without my jumper and I felt suddenly weak, like all my limbs were made of jelly.

Back at the ambulance, we were all given blankets. Me and Agnes sat on the sea wall while Hattie was checked over. A small crowd had gathered, all whispering and pointing, with a couple taking pictures. How sick is that?

'We want to take her to the hospital to check her over,' the paramedic said. 'Is there someone you can ring, to let them know what's happened?'

Agnes and I looked at each other. 'Auntie Sadie,' I said and searched for her number. I had no idea how to get in contact with anyone else who knew Hattie.

'Bayview Bed and Breakfast,' came Auntie Sadie's voice.

'Err, hi.' How exactly are you supposed to tell people news like this? 'It's Jake? I'm staying there? With Hattie?'

'Hi, Jake,' she said, her voice more serious now. 'Everything OK?'

'Yes and no. It is now. I think.'

'Best explain everything.'

'Right. Yes. Of course. Well, it's Hattie. She got stuck in the sinking sand, at the far end of the beach. And the tide was coming in. And, well, Agnes helped her and I called 999. Anyway, she's in the ambulance now, but they want to take her to the hospital to check her over.'

Auntie Sadie swore. 'Are they taking her to Weston Hospital?'

'I think so, yeah.'

'I'll be right there. Thanks for calling me, Jake.'

CHAPTER 19

Hospitals are really, really boring places. Seriously. There is nothing to do if you're not ill. There's not much to do if you are ill.

Auntie Sadie had arrived, hugged us both, and disappeared to find Hattie. Jake and I sat in the waiting room, wrapped in our blankets.

'I'm starving,' I said. 'I'm considering raiding the food bank donations box in a minute.'

Jake looked at me sideways. 'Seriously?'

'I'm seriously hungry.'

'Other than being really hungry, are you OK? I mean, you did something pretty scary just now.'

I frowned. It hadn't been scary. Not really. It had been necessary.

'I did what was needed,' I said, in the end.

'Yes,' said Jake slowly. 'But not everyone would have done that.'

'I'm not everyone.'

Jake smiled. 'No. You're not.'

'Can I ask you a question?'

'Sure.'

'The test we did before we came. You lied, didn't you?'

Jake's smile vanished. He didn't say anything for a moment.

'I know you lied. The results were really clear. You tried to cover it up, but it didn't work. What's wrong with you?'

'Ah, there you are,' said Auntie Sadie from across the waiting room. She had her arm round a very pale-looking Hattie. I was about to push Jake to answer, when he stood up and walked over to them both.

'Everything OK?' His voice sounded different somehow.

'Yes, all fine,' said Auntie Sadie, smiling a big smile. 'What she needs now is a hot bath and an early night.'

'What *I* need now is a meal. What's for tea?' I said.

'We'll sort something out when we get in. I left

in a bit of hurry. Only had time to shout to Parveen that I was going and run out of the door.'

Well, that sucked. I was starving.

We walked out to the minibus which Auntie Sadie had 'parked' outside. Abandoned more like. Three wheels were on the pavement.

Hattie didn't say anything the whole way back and, once at Bayview, she quietly followed her aunt, who said she'd run a bath for her after she'd rung her mum, who was apparently 'freaking out'.

I went to get changed. Getting my clothes off was tricky; they were stuck to me and I had to peel off my jeans. Sand had somehow got inside them. I decided a warm shower would be good, so went and stood under the steamy jet until I'd warmed up.

I had just sat down on my bed, in my warmest jumper and fluffy slippers, when there was a knock at the door.

'Can I come in?' Jake's voice came from outside.

'Sure.'

He poked his head round. He'd changed too.

'Auntie Sadie says it's nearly dinner.'

'About time,' I said, bouncing off the bed.

In the dining room, all the tables had been pushed together. Auntie Sadie stood beside the now massive table in the centre of the room.

'What's going on?' I asked.

Auntie Sadie smiled. 'Parveen has cooked. She got Mr Fitzgerald to help.'

Parveen bustled into the dining room. 'Sit down, sit down,' she said, a massive smile on her face. 'It's a bit of a different suppertime tonight.'

'I can see that,' I said.

Hattie came in. She was wearing her jeans and a big jumper. Her hair, still wet from her bath, was pulled back into a simple ponytail, the odd curl pinging free.

'And now Hattie is here, let's eat,' said Parveen.

Music to my ears. Hattie sat down next to me and Jake sat beside her.

Once everyone was sitting and Marjorie and Marian had stopped arguing, Parveen tinged her glass.

'I just want to say how very pleased we all are that you are all right, Hattie. We were all so worried about you when Sadie rushed out. And so, a toast. To Hattie!'

We all raised our glasses. Bit odd, but there we go.

'To Hattie!' everyone said, and sipped their drinks.

'And to Agnes and Jake for their quick thinking and bravery,' said Auntie Sadie, raising her glass again.

'To Agnes and Jake.'

'Good job,' added Mr Fitzgerald.

'And now for the food.'

Parveen brought out dish after dish of the most amazing food ever. A slow cooked chilli with fajitas, guacamole, soured cream, nachos and cheesy potato skins. We helped ourselves, heaping it onto our plates before tucking in. It. Was. Delicious.

'This is wonderful, Parveen,' Auntie Sadie kept saying. She wasn't wrong. Though I didn't get why, when she was eating such wonderful food, Auntie Sadie was wiping a tear away. Why cry when the food is good?

Hattie was really quiet. For someone who usually never shuts up, it felt strange. Not unpleasant, just odd. Jake was concentrating hard on his food. Auntie Sadie was busy chatting to Parveen about recipes, and even Marjorie and Marian had called a truce and were chatting to Mr Fitzgerald about their day.

It was weird. Usually I hated noisy groups of people. Mainly because they didn't include me. But this was different. Even though I wasn't talking or laughing with them, it felt like I was still included.

Like if I wanted to join in, that was fine. But if I didn't, that was fine too. It was fine. All just fine.

CHAPTER 20

Hattie

We left the adults to it. Parveen had been at the cooking sherry, Mr Fitzgerald said, and had got very giggly.

We piled into our room. I sat on my bed and wrapped my duvet around me. It was hard to get rid of the cold feeling. I'd warmed up, sort of, but my bones were still cold. Like I had rods of ice stuck through me. The phone call with Mum was playing over and over in my head. She'd sobbed down the phone. I'd told her it hadn't been that big a deal. No need to make it worse.

Agnes sat on the desk chair and Jake lay on Agnes' bed. No one was really talking. It's like we're too tired to say anything. But there was so much to say.

When you have so much to say, how do you start?

'So,' I said. 'Busy day, huh?'

'Not especially,' said Agnes. 'I got zero revision done. And then I sat for hours doing nothing at the hospital.'

You can count on Agnes to set me straight.

'Look, I wanted to say, I'm, well, I'm sorry.'

I took a deep breath.

'I'm sorry I said all that stuff before. I was angry and so I said things I didn't mean.'

'That's OK,' said Agnes.

'It really isn't,' I insisted. 'I wasn't even angry with you guys. Not really.'

'You weren't?' said Jake. 'Cos it kinda sounded like you were.'

I sighed. It was complicated.

'No. It was something else.'

'Was it something on your phone?' asked Agnes. 'I bet it was. You're always angry after you've looked at your phone.'

'Well, sort of. It's Zara, Chelsea and Scarlett...'

'They're your friends, right? I vaguely remember you going on about them on the bus.'

'Well, yeah. Someone's said something about me. It isn't true, but they've believed it. And now they're not talking to me.'

'Don't sound much like friends to me,' said Jake.

'Oh, they are. They just do this sometimes. All I've got to do is figure out a way to prove I didn't do what they think I did.'

'What did they say you did?'

I sighed.

'They think I kissed Scarlett's boyfriend. At a party.'

'Why do they think that?' asked Jake.

'Because Bailey kissed me. I shut it down, straight away. But someone must have seen us and assumed the rest.'

'And they don't believe you?' Agnes looked shocked. 'Have you told them that you're not lying?'

'Yes, Agnes, I have. Of course.'

'I don't get it then. They believe someone else over you? Their friend?' Agnes shook her head in disbelief. 'Of course you wouldn't have done that. You're not that person.'

Agnes' words caught me off guard. For a moment or two, the lump in my throat threatened to choke me.

'So, what you going to do?' asked Jake.

'Dunno.'

'Still reckon they sound like pretty crappy friends. And I should know,' said Jake.

'What do you mean by that?'

'Oh, I don't mean you guys,' said Jake, back-tracking horribly. 'It was some other people. I thought they were my friends, but as it turns out, they're not.'

'Elaborate,' I said.

Jake sighed. 'I was on the basketball team. We spent all our time together. They were my guys. Turns out we were only teammates. They were supposed to be there for me, no matter what.'

Agnes was frowning at him. 'Aren't they your friends anymore?'

Jake shook his head. 'Nah, they ditched me when I left the squad two weeks ago.'

'Why did you quit?'

Jake hesitated, then looked at Agnes. Understanding was dawning on her face.

'You had to leave because you're ill?' she said.

Jake nodded.

'I knew you'd lied,' she said, clapping her hands together.

Jake didn't look pleased to be found out.

'What's the matter with you?' I asked. 'You don't look sick.'

'I don't know what it is.' He was breathing pretty hard, and his face was glowing. 'It's tough to say.'

'Just say it,' said Agnes. 'Like ripping a plaster off. Hurts like hell, then it's all fine.'

He smiled at her.

'OK, here's the thing. I found a lump. Just really tiny. But since then, I've not been able to think straight. My mind is all over the place. I've got a headache, like, all of the time. My stomach's hurting. It's why I had to pull out before regionals. I can't concentrate on anything.'

'Have you had it checked out?' I asked.

He shook his head.

'What? Jake, seriously, that's what you've got to do.'

'It might be nothing. Something totally normal.'

'Or, it could be something…'

'Fatal?' asked Agnes.

'Agnes! What d'you say that for?'

'Well, that is what you're worried about, isn't it, Jake?'

Jake's voice was strained. 'I guess. I wish it would go away.'

'That sucks,' I said. 'But, seriously, first thing tomorrow, you are booking an appointment at the doctor for when you get home. Or I'm doing it for you.'

Jake nodded. 'OK.'

We were all quiet for a moment.

'Anyway,' said Jake, clearly wanting to lift the mood. 'What about you, Agnes? Me and Hattie have told everyone what's going on. What deep, dark secret do you have?'

I would have bet money Jake was not expecting Agnes to have any kind of secret.

Agnes tilted her head at him. 'I've read about this. We're bonding here, aren't we? Sharing secrets – that's one of the steps towards friendship, isn't it?'

Agnes breaks my heart sometimes. 'Seriously Agnes? You've never had anyone to share secrets with?'

'Not really. I mean, I talk to my sister. But she's not around anymore.'

'No one else?' asked Jake.

'No,' said Agnes simply.

I looked at the girl who had walked into sinking sand for me, who had held my head above water, who had saved me without a moment's hesitation.

'Well, you've got friends now,' I told her. 'Anytime you've got a secret, you can share it with us.'

'Absolutely,' said Jake.

Agnes seemed to weigh us up. 'Well, there is one thing. My sister, Rose, is in Weston and I've been trying to find her. That's the whole reason I wanted to come.'

'What?' I said. 'I thought this was a revision holiday.'

'Nope, that was a cover. It's been horrible at home without her. She needs to come back to live with me and Mum again. Everything's wrong without her, so I've come to find her and tell her she needs to come back.'

'That's the reason you wanted to come to Weston?' said Jake. 'The whole reason we all came?' And he started laughing. 'Why didn't you say? We could have helped you!'

'People aren't usually too interested in giving me help,' said Agnes.

'Well, first thing tomorrow, we're going to start looking.'

Agnes grinned, and I realised that I hadn't often seen her smile.

CHAPTER 21

Jake

Lying in bed later, looking out at the stars through the roof light, I couldn't stop thinking about today. Every time I thought about Hattie and Agnes in the sinking sand, seeing the waves break over them, it made me shiver and goosebumps pop up all over me. It had all been way too real and close.

Agnes had been amazing. I couldn't figure her out at all. So distant one minute, then leaping in to save someone without a second thought the next. Definitely the right way round to be. You don't want friends that abandon you when things get tricky.

Hattie had been quiet all evening. Not surprising really. Seriously intense day. And hearing about what's going on with her friends helps sort of explain why she's been acting off, though I still reckoned she'd be better off without them. One thing I did know: I was going to do everything I could to help Hattie and Agnes. Starting first thing tomorrow, we'd go on a sister-hunt for Agnes. Weston wasn't that massive – it couldn't be impossible to find someone here.

I got out of bed and pushed open the roof light. I could hear cars driving down the road, but a bit further away I could hear the soft noise of waves breaking on the beach. The air was cool. I closed my eyes and concentrated on the sound of the sea. I tried not to think about the doctor's appointment. I was definitely going to book one tomorrow; it was the right thing to do. I'd known that all along really.

I tried to concentrate on Hattie and Agnes and what they'd said to reassure me: that it was likely to be nothing serious; that because it wasn't very big it would be really treatable even if it was something nasty.

I flopped down on my bed, leaving the window open so I could hear the waves. The best way to escape my thoughts was to sleep. Sometimes I wish I could hibernate until I knew the answer. It was this waiting that was slowly killing me.

Next morning was sunny, but cold. My bedroom was extra chilly as I'd fallen asleep with the window open. Hattie was banging on my door.

'Come on! Wake up! It's breakfast time!'

'All right!' I called and turned over. Perhaps a few more minutes.

'Well, be quick. We're going looking for Agnes' sister today and I want to get started.'

Agnes' sister. Of course. I peeled myself out of bed and headed for the shower.

Agnes and Hattie were already at the table when I got to the dining room. Hattie looked better than she had yesterday, like someone had coloured her back in. I went to tell Auntie Sadie what I wanted for breakfast.

'So today is Operation Sister Hunt, then?' I said as I sat down. Agnes grinned.

'Yep,' said Hattie. 'We're not stopping until we've found Rose.'

'Though first,' said Agnes, 'you're booking your doctor's appointment.'

I nodded. 'Definitely doing that today.'

'Straight after breakfast. Get it done,' said Hattie. 'Who are you going to go with?'

I didn't answer straight away. I hadn't really wanted anyone there. But at the same time sort of did.

'If you had a really bad throat infection,' said Agnes, 'who would go with you?'

'My mum,' I said.

Agnes raised her eyebrows at me. I had my answer.

'Best give your mum a call, too,' said Hattie gently. 'I know it's going to be a super-awkward conversation, but better that than her not knowing and not coming with you.'

I knew they were right. But it wasn't the awkwardness that was going to be the worst thing, it was knowing that it would make Mum worry. Ruin her day/week/year/life depending on how things went.

Booking the appointment was fairly straightforward. Hattie insisted I put the phone on speaker so she could check I was doing it right. Agnes was off, getting things ready for the day.

'Is it an urgent problem?' asked the receptionist.

'Um,' I said. I didn't know. Depends on what it is. Hattie was nodding hard at me. 'Yes,' I said.

'And would a telephone appointment be appropriate?' Hattie had switched and was now shaking her head.

'No, I need to see a doctor,' I said.

'Of course,' said the receptionist. 'I've got an appointment on Monday.'

She told me the details. It was all booked.

'Well done,' said Hattie.

I smiled. I felt really shaky. It was suddenly real. Once all these people started knowing, there was no way I could go back to trying to ignore it.

'Now, give your mum a call. While you're on a roll. You'll feel better for having got it done.'

'When did you get so wise?'

Hattie smiled. 'Read it in one of those life-advice books. Do the stuff you least want to do first. Then your day will only get easier, and you'll feel brilliant for having conquered your fears. Sounded sensible.'

'You want to listen to that too?'

'Nah,' she said. 'Reckon that's one for just you and your mum. I'll see you downstairs in a bit.' She got off the chair and left the room, pulling the door gently to behind her.

I took a deep breath. How do you even make a call like this? By just doing it.

'Hi Jake.' She answered after two rings. 'Everything OK?'

It was and it wasn't.

'Sort of. The holiday's all fine. It's just I need to talk to you. About something. The thing is … the thing is…'

I was making a real mess of this.

'I've made a doctor's appointment for Monday. Nothing major. I need to get something checked out, that's all. I'm sure it'll be nothing. But would you come with me? Please?'

'Of course.' Mum sounded confused. 'What are you getting checked out? Don't you feel well?'

I swallowed. My throat felt dry.

'I found a lump. A couple of weeks ago. And it's not going. So I need to check it out.'

Mum was quiet for a moment. I wished I was there with her. Wished I didn't have to tell her this. Wished she never had to hear this.

'That sounds like a very good idea. And you've booked the appointment already?'

'Yes, it's at ten-thirty.'

'Do you want me to come and collect you now?' she said. 'Would that help?'

I thought about it. On one hand, being back at home would be fab, but there would be way too much thinking time between now and Monday. And, besides, I'd promised Agnes I would help look for Rose.

'No thanks, Mum. I'm enjoying it here.'

'Oh, that's good.' I could hear in her voice that she was trying to sound cheerful. 'Well, if that changes, I can come and get you. Any time.'

'Thanks, Mum.'

'No worries.'

'And Mum? Love you.'

Her voice cracked the tiniest bit. She covered it up, but I heard it. 'Love you too, Jakey.'

Ten minutes later, we stood outside the Bayview Bed and Breakfast.

'OK, Agnes,' said Hattie, 'tell us everything you know about Rose. I want details, a photo, anything that might help us find her.'

Agnes pulled out her phone. She showed us a picture of a girl who looked a little like Agnes – same nose and mouth, but with dyed jet-black hair.

'Why is she in Weston?' I asked.

'She's got a temporary job at the council. She'd said she was staying with a friend but, when I went there, her friend said she'd got her own place and had moved out.'

'Did she know where to?' I asked.

Agnes shook her head. 'She said it can't have been far out of the centre, as Rose said she was still able to walk to work, but she didn't know exactly where.'

'So you're sure she's still in Weston?' said Hattie.

Agnes nodded. 'Definitely. This is where her job

is, and I think I saw her, the other night, when we were having milkshakes. I saw her walk past.'

'Was that why you ran out? Why didn't you say?' Hattie demanded.

'It was a secret. Besides, I didn't think you'd care.'

I thought back to that evening. I hadn't even bothered getting up from my chair.

'Well, we care now. Have you got anything else that would help us find her?' I said.

'No.' Agnes shook her head. 'Just that she works at the council.'

'Do you know what she's doing at the council?' asked Hattie.

'No idea. She didn't tell me.'

'Council offices it is, then,' I said.

I was feeling like I had more energy now – Hattie had been right. Despite the call to Mum being hard, I now felt sort of better. I'd done what I'd been dreading, and it hadn't been as bad as I'd imagined, and that felt good.

We walked into town along the seafront, the brisk wind from the Bristol Channel blowing our hair and billowing out our jackets. The sun was out and that only added to my feeling that everything was going to be OK. Who knows? Maybe this lump would turn out to be nothing.

The council office was the other side of the town centre near the station. The town hall looked fairly impressive with arches at the front and a tall clock tower. We pushed open the door and went in.

Agnes must have been nervous because she was doing a thing with her fingers which I'd seen her do before when she was trying to calm down.

Agnes walked up to the front desk. 'Hi,' she said to the receptionist. 'My sister works here. I need to see her.'

'Name?'

'Rose Cronk,' said Agnes.

The woman tapped on a keyboard and studied her screen.

We waited.

'I'm sorry, there's no one here by that name.'

'There must be,' said Agnes. 'She works at the council.'

The woman frowned at Agnes. 'Well, there is no one in this building today by that name.'

Agnes was struggling to keep calm.

'Check again! You must have missed her. Did you spell Cronk right? It's C-R-O-N-K.'

'I spelled it correctly,' said the woman, coldly.

Agnes was about to speak again, when Hattie butted in.

'It's really very important. We've had some rather shocking family news, and we wanted to break it to her in person. I hope you understand.'

The woman's face changed. 'There is somewhere else I could look. It might be she's not based at these offices.' Her nails tapped again on the keyboard.

Hattie smiled at Agnes.

'Ah, yes. Here she is. Rose Cronk. She works at the museum.'

CHAPTER 22

The museum was tucked down a backstreet, and looked like it was in a few converted old houses.

I marched up to the front desk and nodded at the lady behind the computer. 'Hello. Do you have a Rose Cronk working here?'

The woman paused. 'I'm afraid we can't give out private information.'

'What? Who works here isn't private information. I just want to know if she works here. That's all. It's very important.'

'I'm sorry,' said the woman firmly. 'But I can't tell you that.'

Why did no one understand? I needed to see Rose. I needed her like I needed air and water and life.

'BUT I WANT TO SPEAK TO ROSE.'

Why wouldn't she let me? It was just a little thing. It wasn't going to hurt anyone. I could even wait until Rose's lunch hour, so it wouldn't stop her working.

'Come on,' said Hattie, gently pulling my arm. 'Leave it.'

'BUT I DON'T WANT TO LEAVE IT. I WANT TO SPEAK TO ROSE.'

Jake was on my other side. 'Drop it, Agnes, we'll find another way.'

They ushered me out, me still giving evils to the woman at the desk over my shoulder. Who did she think she was?

'You can't just go barging up to someone like that,' said Hattie, once we were back outside. 'You'll get people's backs up.'

'All she had to do was tell me whether Rose works here or not. It's not a tricky question.'

'It's not because she didn't understand,' Jake said. 'She just didn't know what you wanted.'

I shook my head. 'Then she's incredibly thick. I told her exactly what I wanted. I wanted to know if Rose works there.'

Hattie took a deep breath. 'She didn't know *why* you wanted to know.'

'It's none of her business.'

'But you could have been a crazy person. She was protecting Rose.'

'I'm not crazy.'

'I know that,' said Hattie. 'But she doesn't.'

Huh. People are really confusing sometimes.

'Look,' said Jake, 'I've got another idea. Let's see if we can find Rose ourselves.'

'I suppose it is free to get in,' said Hattie. 'We could have a look around for her.'

Jake grinned. 'Come on then. Act natural and it'll be fine.'

He walked up to the front desk. 'Three for the museum, please.'

The woman thinned her eyes at him, but he smiled widely back.

She handed over three tickets. 'You guys too old to do our treasure-hunt quiz?'

'It's fine, thanks,' said Hattie, 'we've got our own treasure hunt.'

We followed Jake through the gift shop and out into a covered courtyard, with a café at the end. It smelt of frying and coffee and was filled with small kids, all shouting and arguing over which Fruit Shoot was theirs.

Above us, natural light was streaming in from massive glass panels in the roof. It was all set up like an old cobbled street. Around the edges were tables for the café and kids' activities.

'Now let's get searching,' said Jake. 'Can I have another look at her picture? And be careful. Don't do anything to get yourselves noticed. Agnes, that means you.'

'Of course,' I said, showing him Rose's photo. 'I'll blend right in.'

We walked to the back of the courtyard and into one of the smaller rooms. There was a film playing with a couple of benches in front of the screen. I edged along the side of the wall, feeling like a spy going under cover.

'What are you doing?' hissed Hattie.

'I'm being inconspicuous.'

'Like hell you are. Just walk normally.'

The staff member in there was not Rose. We moved on to the next room and the next. No Rose. We tried upstairs among the photo galleries, near the timelines, we even spent quite a time in the dressing-up area. Jake tried on a top hat and Hattie an old-fashioned bonnet. I didn't fancy it. How many people must have tried them on before?

After about thirty minutes, we still hadn't found

Rose. We studied a map and double-checked we'd been into every bit of the museum. Jake picked a bench to sit on, and Hattie flopped down next to him.

I stood in front of them. 'What are you doing? We can't stop. We've got to break into the offices or something.'

Jake shook his head. 'It might be her day off, Agnes. We can try again tomorrow.'

'But I don't want to come back tomorrow. I want to find her today.'

'It's only one day. It won't make any difference,' said Hattie. 'And besides, she's not here. You can't find her if she's not here.'

My fingers were itching. I tried my 'rubbing thumb and fingers together' trick, but it wasn't working like it usually did. I wanted Rose. I wanted her NOW. I wanted to tell her to COME HOME and I didn't want to wait ANYMORE.

Jake and Hattie looked at each other, then at me.

'Agnes, you've got to calm down. People are staring.'

But I couldn't calm down. I didn't want to calm down. I wanted Rose.

'Listen,' said Jake. 'I've had an idea. She might

be on a coffee break. Why don't we have something to drink in the café before having another search? How does that sound? Only please stop shouting. That woman from reception is giving us funny looks.'

I hadn't even realised I'd been shouting.

CHAPTER 23

Hattie

Agnes can be pretty terrifying when she's angry. I mean, I get that it's infuriating that she can't find her sister, but I also get where the woman from reception was coming from. But Agnes seemed to calm down after we moved to the café.

I was checking to see if I had enough money to upgrade my hot chocolate to a deluxe one, when Agnes spotted her.

'Rose! She's over there!'

'Where?' Both Jake and I were searching all round, trying to see where Agnes was looking.

'She's behind the counter.'

Of course. The one place we hadn't checked, because it was on the way out, was the café.

I didn't think Rose would need telling where

Agnes was. Most people within a half-mile radius now knew where Agnes was.

Rose stared at us, her eyes fixed on Agnes, a look of complete shock on her face. She spoke to the other person who was working with her, tipping her head in our direction. The woman glanced our way briefly before nodding.

Rose took off her apron and came over to us.

'Agnes, what are you doing here?'

She looked like Agnes, same grey eyes.

'I'm here to tell you to come home,' said Agnes. 'Do you have a bag you need to get? We can go right now.'

'Agnes. Stop. I can't come with you now. I'm at work.'

'But now you know I need you at home, you're going to stop working.'

'No, Agnes. I work here, and I live in Weston now.'

'But it's all wrong. Nothing feels right at home without you.'

Rose's face was calm.

'I know. And I'm sorry that's how you feel. But it'll get better.'

'No, it won't. Mum doesn't stack the dishwasher like you do. And she's messy. I need you to come back. Please. Please come back. I've found you a job. One near our house so you don't have to live somewhere else.'

Agnes fished around in her pocket until she pulled out a crumpled piece of paper. 'See. No one else is going to apply for it because I've got the only advert. It's at the corner shop. It's perfect.'

Agnes' face was shining with hope. I knew Rose wasn't going to come back but Agnes clearly didn't know. I hadn't realised Rose was such a big part of Agnes' life. This was the reason she'd come here, the whole reason any of us had come to Weston for the week. All because Agnes wanted Rose to come home. How had I not known she was so important to Agnes?

'Hi.' I stepped forward. 'I'm Hattie.'

Rose looked surprised. 'Hattie?'

'Yes, Agnes' friend. And this is her other friend, Jake.'

Rose looked completely bewildered as she shook both our hands. 'Nice to meet you,' she said. 'Look, I'm sorry, but who are you?'

'We're Agnes' friends,' said Jake. 'We've been helping her to find you.'

Rose looked properly shocked now.

'She's been desperate to see you,' I said. 'Least you could do is have a cup of tea with her.'

Agnes nodded. Rose sighed and looked at her watch.

'I've got half an hour.'

Rose got us all hot chocolates from the café and we sat around one of the tables on the cobbled indoor street. The rain was hammering on the roof lights above us.

'So? You've come all the way to Weston, hey?' said Rose putting down the tray of drinks.

Agnes nodded.

'Mum know you're here?'

'Not exactly. She thinks we're in Blackpool.'

Rose snorted and blew on her hot chocolate. She picked off one of the marshmallows and ate it.

'I do miss you, you know,' she said.

'Then why can't you come home?' said Agnes. 'Is it the job I found? It's not good enough, is it?'

'No, it's not the job. That was really thoughtful of you.' Rose sighed. 'It's because sometimes things have to change. And it's hard when they do. But then it gets easier. You get used to it. And, in the long run, it's better. I know that's hard to understand.'

Agnes was shaking her head slowly. 'But...? But I thought it was only for a couple of months. That's bad enough. But you sound like you're staying longer. I hate not knowing where you are. Or what you are doing. When you were at home, I knew where you were every second. I knew that you were at college on a Tuesday and studying at the library on a Wednesday and you cooked lasagne on Thursdays and helped me with my English homework on a Saturday. I knew everything. And now I know nothing.'

'Would it help, knowing a bit more?' said Rose softly.

'It might. But probably not,' said Agnes.

Rose began to talk, and while she talked, she wrote on a napkin with a Weston Museum pen. She talked about her shift patterns, her new house, the friends she now lived with, the route she walked to work, which bars she liked going to in the evenings, which nights she cooked in her shared house and what the view out of her window was like. All three of us listened. It was like downloading someone's whole life. Agnes stopped her every now and again to ask questions: 'Which supermarket do you go to? Is the chippy as good as the one at home? Who do you share a house with?' and Rose answered every single one.

'How's that?' asked Rose, when she'd finished.

Agnes considered for a moment. 'It's OK. But I'm right, aren't I? This isn't a temporary job, is it?'

Rose shook her head. 'I'm so sorry, Agnes. Mum thought it would be too unsettling for you while you had exams, and we didn't want to upset you.'

'I knew there was something that didn't make sense,' said Agnes.

'I really am sorry,' said Rose. 'But now you know, we can make plans for you to come and visit once your exams are over.'

Agnes smiled. 'It's not quite the same, but that would be nice. Would you make your lasagne?'

Rose laughed. 'Of course!'

Agnes smiled again.

'So.' Rose turned her attention to me and Jake. 'How come you're in Weston?'

Agnes beamed. 'Well, they've both got their own stuff going on.'

Rose raised an eyebrow. 'Really?'

'Hattie here has problems with her friends not talking to her. She says they've "ghosted" her. Not sure exactly what that means.'

'Ghosted, huh? That's not very nice. You sure they're your friends?'

'That's what I said,' said Jake, butting in.

'Yeah, thanks for that,' I said, giving him a look.

'And what about you?' Rose turned to him.

'Fancied some sea air.'

Clearly, he didn't want to share.

'Oh, Jake's ill. Not sure what with yet. Might be bad. Right, Jake?'

Jake's face drained, but he nodded. 'Thanks for the reminder, Agnes.'

'Had you forgotten?' Agnes sounded confused.

'Maybe nearly, for a moment,' he replied.

Rose clearly had no idea what to do with this random information, about her sister's random friends. 'Well, I hope it works out for both of you.' She checked her watch. 'I gotta get back to work.' She looked like she wanted to hug Agnes, but in the end, just patted her arm.

'Look after yourself, kid.'

CHAPTER 24

Jake

Agnes' sister was nice. You could tell she totally got where Agnes was coming from. I don't. Not all the time. The more time I spend with her, though, the more I understand her. She's not mean on purpose. In fact, I don't think she's mean at all. None of what she says is meant cruelly. She just says it like it is. One of the world's straight talkers.

Agnes is the one who is most open, most honest and most uncomplicated about what I've got going on. She's not dodging the issue, or avoiding the subject. She's been researching my symptoms, too. She mentioned it in passing over breakfast.

We walked into town and found a café. Agnes went to buy us all a cup of tea while Hattie and me found us a booth to sit in. Hattie was checking her phone and I could almost see her folding in on herself.

'Everything OK?'

She jumped. Her eyes were wet.

'Yeah,' she said. She was lying.

I raised my eyebrows. 'Really?'

'OK, it's not OK. It's just…' She struggled to find the words. 'It's just, it's rubbish watching them. You know. Having a great time without me.'

'Is it too simplistic to say don't look?'

'They're tagging me in all their photos. Every time I look at my phone, there are loads of messages.'

'Ugh. That sucks.' I paused. 'Makes you want to turn it round, doesn't it?'

Agnes arrived with the teas, and some cakes. 'What sucks?'

'Hattie's "friends" are trying to make her jealous that she's missing out on their wonderful Easter holidays.'

Agnes snorted. 'The laugh will be on them when they realise they haven't been revising.'

'I'm not sure they'll think like that,' said Hattie. She broke off a piece of cake and popped it into her mouth.

'You're feeling sad, right?' said Agnes.

Hattie rolled her eyes but nodded.

'And it would be better if they felt sad?'

'Not sad, exactly. They are my friends after all.'

'Yeah,' I interrupted. 'We want them to feel sad.'

'Not sad,' insisted Hattie. 'Just like they might be missing out on the wonderful time I'm having. Which is what I've been trying to do.'

We looked around the greasy spoon café, with the rain plopping down outside and the steamed-up windows.

'Well, there's a lot to be jealous of,' I said, seriously. Hattie grinned.

Agnes was frowning. 'You've been trying to do all the "usual" Instagram shots. You've got to make it more Weston-y.'

'What do you mean?' said Hattie.

'Your Instagram has to have a Weston-super-Mare makeover. You've got to show what an amazing time you're having here because of all the weird and wonderful things in Weston.' She frowned. 'Not sure exactly what that looks like. I'm guessing it's not quite like mine?'

She showed us her phone – it was a catalogue of every textbook she'd read.

'Probably not,' Hattie laughed. 'But I like your

thinking. It's the candyfloss and the pier and the sea and the history.'

'It's got to include a donkey ride,' I said. 'You can't come to Weston and not go on the donkeys.'

Agnes smiled.

'I'd like that actually.' Hattie was nodding.

We worked out a list (Agnes' idea) for the day we had left before we went home. We had to cram in as much as we could. Like we were banking up the experiences.

It was only when I got into bed that night, I thought if everything didn't turn out well with my doctor's appointment, I'd be looking back on these experiences in a different light too.

CHAPTER 25

My alarm went off early the next morning. I'd worked out the schedule the night before. If we were going to get everything done today, we'd need some serious dedication. I checked over the itinerary. Shower, dress, breakfast. I'd checked with Auntie Sadie that we could have it earlier than usual, so we could make an early start.

I shook Hattie.

'Gerroff,' she mumbled and rolled over. I shook her again.

'It's time to get up, Hattie. We've got a lot planned.'

'What time is it?'

'Six.'

'What? That's ridiculous. Wake me up in three hours.'

I kept on shaking and she eventually gave up trying to sleep and staggered into the bathroom. I could see she was going to be our weakest link today. Hopefully she'd remember what we were trying to do.

After breakfast, which I photographed extensively, we headed out. Luckily the sun was shining.

'Perfect light.' I checked a test photo I'd taken of Bob the gnome. 'Really brings out the colours.'

'Great,' said Hattie.

'Let's have a look,' asked Jake. 'We ought to post the pictures as we go. For maximum effect.'

'They've got to be on your account, though, Hattie. I don't want to mess mine up.'

Hattie seemed to wake up at that. 'I'm not putting a photo of a gnome on my account. I know things are desperate, but I have standards.'

'Like what?' I had my rules for my account, but from what I could see from Hattie's account, she didn't have any.

'Rule one: it's got to be cool.'

I rolled my eyes. Sooooo indefinable.

'Look,' said Hattie, 'I'll know it when I see it. You keep taking photos and I'll pick the best for my Instagram. Deal?'

'Deal.' To be honest, I was glad I didn't have to make the decisions.

I snapped Jake and Hattie as they chatted over what we were going to do first. Hattie was pulling a funny face and Jake was waving his arms about. Probably not cool.

'OK, open-top bus first,' said Jake.

We walked along the seafront and caught the bus. It whooshed along. We were the only ones on the top, as it was still early and quite chilly. Hattie's hair was whipping round her face. Got a great shot of her hair wrapped round her nose.

'You've got to delete it, I look awful,' she said. Jake laughed but Hattie glared at him.

'Think arty,' she said to me. 'It's all in the filter.'

I took a couple more and she picked one where her hair was swished across her face, her eyes were looking straight into the camera, and she looked like she *might* smile. She liked that one and added it to her Insta.

We got off the bus at Uphill and walked across the sandy grass area to a hummock overlooking the sea. The breeze had dropped and the sun was coming out.

We stopped. The sea was in and the sunlight made the usually murky waters take on a glimmer. Like a black diamond.

Jake breathed in a deep breath and let it out slowly. 'It's wonderful here,' he said. 'I wish we didn't have to go home.'

I was going to say something about that not being possible, but Hattie said, 'Yeah, me too.'

They both stood, smiling at the horizon. I couldn't hold myself back any longer.

'But think of the practicalities – where would we sit our exams? What if we missed them completely? Hattie, I thought you were missing your friends. And Jake, you'd have to find a local doctor double-quick if you moved down here.'

Jake stopped grinning. So did Hattie.

'Of course, you're right, Agnes,' Jake agreed. 'It would be a real headache.'

'We don't really mean it,' said Hattie.

'Why say it if you don't mean it?'

Jake shrugged. 'I guess it's like a wish. If a genie gave you three wishes, and as part of those wishes, he sorted out all those practical problems too. It's that kind of wish. I know I can't, but I'd really like to.'

I nodded. That sort of made sense. And a genie would definitely think of everything.

I lifted my phone up. 'Selfie.' We all leaned together, squinting in the sunshine, and I pressed the button. Hattie wouldn't want that one. It had me and Jake in it.

We walked back along the promenade, stopping for candyfloss near the pier. Hattie posed again with hers and found that wistful, half-smile again. Jake pushed the back of her head, just as I took the shot, and she went face-deep in pink sugar. I kept taking as Hattie re-emerged and chased Jake onto the beach and put a handful of sand down his back.

'Aagghh, I've got sand in my boxers now,' he shouted, jiggling his legs and shaking the top of his jeans.

Hattie looked pleased with herself. 'Well, you should have thought about that before you decided to give me a floss facial,' she said. 'I've got it in my hair.' She chewed on the end of a clump of hair. 'Still tastes good, though.'

At lunchtime we stopped by the museum and Rose came and sat with us on the beach. I didn't stop taking pictures. That was my job today, and I was going to do it well.

'What are you doing this afternoon?' she asked.

'Dunno exactly,' said Hattie.

I knew exactly. The list was in my back pocket.

'I know what you should do,' said Rose. 'Everyone has to do it when they come to Weston.

Play the two-penny slots. Have a pound each, and no more. See who can come out with the most money.'

That sounded ridiculous. I knew the odds on those things. The way to come out with the most money would be not to put a single coin in a single machine. And possibly look out for dropped coins.

'Sounds brilliant,' said Jake. 'I'm up for it, if you guys are? Does it fit with your look, Hattie?'

Rose groaned. 'You're not still chasing after those friends, are you? Listen, ditch them. They're not worth it. You've got to be you. And you've got to find people who like you for who you are, not what your Instagram looks like.'

'Easy for you to say,' said Hattie. 'You don't have to worry about that stuff. You're old.'

Rose snorted. 'Yeah. Twenty-one is really ancient. Look, go do the two-penny machines. I'll even give you the three quid you need.'

So we did. I followed my strategy and came out the clear winner, with a pound and two pence. Jake lost everything but declared himself rich in life, after getting the giggles watching Hattie get so into it.

Hattie thought she'd lost everything, too, but with her last coin, a whole stack that had been teetering on the edge fell and she came away with thirty-eight pence. She too said she'd won, because she'd had the fun of playing *and* still had some money left.

It wasn't until we were back at Bayview that we realised none of the shots from the pier were Instagram shots. Hattie was smiling in all of them.

CHAPTER 26

Hattie

Auntie Sadie had made the decision to keep all the tables together in the dining room. She said she liked that we were her big family. It was our last night at Bayview, and Parveen and Mr Fitzgerald were going the next day as well. Only Marjorie and Marian were staying on for another week.

'You youngsters will have to come back again next year,' said Parveen. 'It's what me and Giles do.'

Mr Fitzgerald smiled. 'That's how good friendships work. Doesn't matter how long you're apart. You can pick right up where you left off.'

Parveen was nodding. 'Have you had a good week?'

Agnes answered first. 'Not nearly enough

revision. I'm going to have to really step it up a gear next week if I'm going to get it all done.'

'That sounds like it's been a very good week, if you've not had time to revise,' said Parveen smiling. I could tell Agnes didn't really agree, but amazingly she didn't say anything.

'How about you, Jake?' said Mr Fitzgerald. 'Good week?'

'Yeah, brilliant.' He didn't say anything else. I guessed he wasn't quite ready to tell anyone about what was going on with him. And I got it. I didn't think I would want to either.

'It's been a great day today,' I said, smiling at the thought of everything we'd done. It was true, and it wasn't until I said it that I realised I'd not had a really great day in a long time.

After supper, we walked down to the sea and along the promenade in the direction of the Old Pier, round the headland to a small pebbly beach. I couldn't quite face the sand again and I was pleased to see the sea was on its way out, with waves gently breaking right down at the bottom of an old jetty. We climbed up onto a high rock and perched, and threw stones into a rock pool.

'Who can hit that big rock, the one by the slipway?' said Jake, pointing.

'I bet I can,' I said, gathering a handful of pebbles. I threw one. It missed. Agnes threw one and so did Jake. They missed too.

'So, another week before school starts, and another three weeks, then it's exams,' I said.

'I keep forgetting about the exams,' said Jake.

'How can you forget about the exams? I know it is 734 hours and 27 minutes until my first exam,' said Agnes.

'Got other things to think about,' muttered Jake.

'Do you want to talk about it?' I asked. Jake had spent the last couple of days making sure that Agnes found her sister and that I had a good time and, more importantly, had good photos.

He shrugged. 'Not sure it helps. I mean, it won't change anything. I'll still have to wait to see the doctor on Monday.'

'Talking about stuff doesn't work for me,' said Agnes matter-of-factly. 'But I've read lots of studies that say it's beneficial. You could try it. Kind of like an experiment. What have you got to lose?'

Jake half-smiled. 'It could make me feel worse?'

Agnes shook her head. 'Unlikely.'

Jake started talking. And he didn't stop. He told us how he's been feeling since he'd found the lump.

That he wished it would go away. That he tried not to think about it, but the harder he tried, the more the thoughts were there, in everything he was doing.

'It was like the more I tried to ignore it, the more I couldn't. Everything got interrupted by it. It's why I had to come off the team. Couldn't concentrate. And I didn't want to let the team down by ... being rubbish.'

'I'm sure you wouldn't have been rubbish,' said Agnes.

Jake looked over at her. 'Thanks, but I wouldn't have been great.'

'Do the others know why you cancelled?'

'Nah. I said something about wanting to concentrate on my exams.'

'How did they take that?'

'Fine,' Jake shrugged. 'They don't get into things like your friends do. But they haven't included me in anything since. I'm off the WhatsApp group; no more team updates. It's no biggie. I get it. I'm not on the team anymore so don't get to join in with team stuff. Only some of them I've been playing with since year seven, that's all.'

He rubbed his hand over his head. 'Do you think they'll biopsy?'

The words hung in the evening air.

'Are you worried it might hurt?' I asked.

'Sort of. I'm more worried about what it might find. I want to try and keep thinking it'll all be fine. That it's just some weird cyst that will clear up one day. But my brain won't let me. It always pulls towards the worst case...' His voice trailed off. 'And it doesn't help that my head won't stop hurting. What if that means it's not just a lump, it's now spread.'

Why does no one ever tell you what to say in these situations? Why is the best advice always 'just be there for them'? How useless is that? I scrabbled around in my brain, trying desperately to find something that would take away his pain. Make it all OK. But I had nothing.

'I'm so sorry, Jake,' I said. 'That sucks. Are there any of your mates you could talk to?'

'Nah. Not sure I could handle telling them.'

So Jake had no one. I frowned. He was seriously in need of some friends.

Agnes had been quietly watching Jake, but now she was busy tapping on her phone. This wasn't really her thing.

'They won't biopsy,' said Agnes, looking up from her phone. 'They might want blood tests, or a urine sample, or they might do an ultrasound. But no biopsy.'

Jake whooshed out a deep breath.

'Thanks, Agnes. That's good to know. I think I'm doing the right thing, this doctor's appointment. I need to know. One way or the other. Good or bad.'

There was nothing I could say so I hugged him, awkwardly, because we were sitting on a rock. And I felt Agnes patting us both on the shoulder.

'Cheers,' said Jake, clearing his throat. 'Perhaps talking isn't such a bad idea.'

CHAPTER 27

Jake

My head was thumping as we walked back from the beach. That worried me. Even though chatting to Hattie and Agnes had made me feel better, my head still hurt. Perhaps that's where it's spread to. Perhaps that's where the battle will actually take place, not a lump, but a shadow on my brain. I shook my head. I had to stop thinking like that. But how? I rubbed my head with my hands. If only the pain would stop, I would be able to think clearly. That might be an upside to knowing – the doctors would be able to get rid of the pain. If you could call it an upside.

We got back to the bed and breakfast. It had turned really cold and the chill was nipping at my fingers and ears. Agnes yawned, and Hattie caught it and yawned too.

'Wow, I'm knackered,' said Hattie.

'High-impact Instagraming does that to you,' Agnes said. She looked at the clock in the hall. 'If I get to bed in the next half an hour, I'll get eight hours' sleep.'

'Can't pass the opportunity of a full eight hours,' said Hattie, grinning. 'Night, Jake.' She and Agnes walked towards their room.

'Night,' I called back. There was no point in going to bed now. I already knew I wouldn't sleep. Perhaps there was something to read in the bookroom. I walked down the corridor and pushed open the door. Mr Fitzgerald was snoozing in one of the armchairs, the soft glow from the lamp and fire illuminating his slipped newspaper. I tiptoed backwards, not wanting to disturb him.

'It's all right, lad,' he said, not opening his eyes.

'Sorry, I didn't know you were in here.'

He opened his eyes and smiled. 'Shouldn't really nap in the evening, but it's hard not too when the food's so good, and the fire's lit.'

I stood in the doorway, not knowing whether to stay or go.

'Come on in. Don't let me stop you.'

I edged my way into the room and walked

over to the paperback whodunnit shelves. I didn't think I'd read any of them, so wondered where to start.

Mr Fitzgerald adjusted his reading glasses and shook out his newspaper.

He'd really helped before, when I was feeling confused. I wanted to thank him. Not in an overly emotional way like you see on the internet, just a thank you.

'Sorry, Mr Fitzgerald, can I disturb you again?'

He put his paper down and looked at me over his glasses.

'Anytime. I have more than enough time on my own since my wife died.'

He waved at the armchair opposite, and I sat down. Bramble, who was sleeping under the chair, snuffled in his sleep.

'I wanted to say thanks for the chat the other day. You were right. I did know what I had to do. I thought I didn't, but I did.'

Mr Fitzgerald nodded. 'That's often the way. It took me a long time to realise that, but it's helped me ever since. Doesn't make it easier to do, but takes away that terrible feeling of indecision.'

I got it. I'd felt a huge weight lifted from fighting the indecision.

'I did the thing. I don't know how it'll work out yet, but I'm already glad I'm doing it.'

'Well, I'm pleased. What are your plans for the rest of the evening?'

'Don't reckon I can sleep just yet, so thought I'd find something to read, but I'm not sure which to choose.'

'Fancy another game of chess? That nap's really woken me up.'

I smiled. 'Yeah, I'd like that. I'd like that a lot.'

We moved a small table, found the board and set out the pieces.

'OK, prepare to be defeated,' said Mr Fitzgerald, rubbing his hands together.

'Don't they say pride goes before a fall?' I said, grinning.

Mr Fitzgerald chuckled. 'Don't they also say game on?'

We played for ages, and Parveen joined us, whispering hints to me when I got cornered. By the time I got into bed that night, my headache had nearly disappeared. I didn't know what that meant but, fortunately, I was so tired, I didn't have long to care.

The following morning, I was woken by Agnes knocking on my door.

'Jake! It's time to get up. You've got to pack, have breakfast and be downstairs with all your stuff by nine forty-five. Our train is at ten-thirty and I don't want to be late. Jake! Have you heard me?'

'Yes!' I called. 'I've heard you.'

'It's only you've not got long. It's nine already.'

Really? I must have slept really well.

'I'll be right down.'

I quickly got dressed and rammed my clothes into my holdall. Giving a quick scan around the room to make sure I'd got everything, I opened the door. I'd enjoyed my week here. I wondered if I'd ever come back.

CHAPTER 28

I'd eaten my breakfast, packed my bags, got my Friday snack of a flask of mocha coffee and some satsumas ready for the train and was sitting in the reception area. I had strong suspicions that Hattie was still not dressed, she'd not had breakfast and was nowhere near packed. I'd had to pick my way across the floor in our room which was strewn with clothes and make-up.

I looked at my phone, flicking through the photos. I'd taken some of Rose and I lingered over those. I still wanted to have her at home rather than here. I sighed.

A sigh echoed near me, and the next second a heavy black Labrador's head nudged its way onto my knee. I froze as Bramble settled himself. What was I supposed to do now? I didn't need to get up from the chair at the moment, but I would want to at some point. Hattie had said over and over that he was a softy, but I'd never quite believed it. How could something so big be soft?

I patted his head very, very gently, so as not to annoy him. He felt warm. And his ears felt silky smooth. He sighed again.

'Do you like that?' I whispered. I had no idea why I was talking to him. He was a dog, of course he couldn't answer. But I was wrong. He could answer. The gentle thud, thud, thud of his tail on the carpet told me he did like it.

'You know what? Being apart from your sister is hard,' I told him. He looked up at me and twitched his eyebrows. 'But I guess you know that. I bet you don't even know where your brothers and sisters are. At least I've got that.'

I left one hand on Bramble's head and texted with the other.

I'm off home this morning. I loved seeing you.

Rose: *It was good to see you too. Looking forward to seeing you after the exams!*

I smiled and pulled at Bramble's ears. As much as I'd miss seeing Rose, I was looking forward to getting home. My routine was in tatters, and my revision had taken a serious hit, especially this last few days. But I had time to pull it back. It would mean a revised revision plan, though. I smiled at the thought. I could colour-code it.

Hattie barged out of our room, lugging her enormous case behind her. 'I think I've got everything, but who knows?' She stopped beside me and rested her case against the wall.

'You've decided to make friends with the hound then?' she said, looking down at me and Bramble.

'I thought I would. But you should have said how lovely he was.' I kept my face serious.

'*What*? I did! Repeatedly. You just…'

I couldn't keep it up any longer and grinned.

'You numpty,' she grinned back. 'I've got to get some breakfast.'

'You've missed it. Breakfast was at eight.'

'I'll beg some toast off Auntie Sadie.'

'And for me too,' called Jake from the stairs. He was hauling his bag down. 'I'm starving.'

It ended up with Hattie and Jake carrying their toast to the van, stuffing our bags into the back, and

197

Auntie Sadie driving faster than I would have liked round corners to get to the station in time.

'Quick, quick,' said Auntie Sadie, as she screeched up to the station, only slightly mounting the kerb. 'I don't think your train's here yet.'

We leaped out, pulling and heaving at our bags.

'I will miss having you all,' she said, giving Hattie a tight hug. 'And good luck with your exams.'

'Cheers for the reminder,' said Hattie, hugging her back.

'Thanks for everything,' said Jake. Auntie Sadie hugged him too.

'Thank you very much,' I said, holding out my hand. Auntie Sadie took it.

'Anytime. Seriously, if you want to come and see your sister, and she can't squeeze you into her place, you give me a call. It would be a pleasure having you to stay again.'

'Really? That would be brilliant.'

Auntie Sadie smiled and patted my hand. 'Now, off you go. You don't want to miss your train.'

We ran to the platform, as our train pulled in.

'Are you sure this is the right train?' I shouted over the noise of whistles and banging doors.

'Yes,' shouted back Hattie. 'Nearly totally.'

'What?' We couldn't get the wrong one, our tickets were non-transferable. We'd be stuck somewhere and have to find our way back and probably have to pay extra.

'I'll check,' said Jake, who asked someone in a uniform.

Once we'd confirmed it was the right train, I relaxed. I was on my way home. I couldn't wait to be back in my own room, at my own house, in my own company.

CHAPTER 29

Hattie

I'd made a promise to myself that I wouldn't look at my phone the whole journey home. Ironically, I'd been so late getting up I hadn't had a chance to look at it before then either. It's weird: your fingers almost get addicted to having your phone there. But I managed it. It was only really hard at the start of the journey. We'd got a table, and my automatic reaction was to reach for my phone.

But then Agnes got out the train picnic and Jake pulled out a pack of cards, so we chatted and munched and played rummy. It was a good job Agnes was looking out, or we would have missed our change. But we made it. Just.

As the train pulled into Manchester Piccadilly, I saw my mum and Ethan waiting for me. It would be good to be home. And still another week before school. Hopefully everyone would have forgotten what had happened at the party by then.

'See you,' I said to Jake and Agnes as we climbed off the train.

'Yeah, see you,' said Jake. 'There's my mum, got to go.'

I watched as Jake walked over to a lady slightly shorter than him. She gave him a big hug and I wondered how much Jake had told her about his doctor's appointment.

'Where's your mum, Agnes?' I asked.

'Oh, she'll be at work. I'm getting the bus home.'

'Really? Are you sure you'll be OK?'

'Absolutely. Even got the right change ready.' She jangled her pocket as proof.

'OK. See you then.'

'See you.'

Agnes walked away across the concourse. I'd see her again on the bus in a week's time. No reason why I should be feeling like I might miss her. But I watched her until I couldn't see her through the crowds anymore.

'Oh, there you are,' said Mum, who immediately hugged me. 'Are you OK? I mean, I know you said you were OK but it's just so good to see you.' She hugged me tighter.

'Everything's totally fine,' I said. 'Nothing to worry about.'

Ethan shoulder bumped me. 'Glad you didn't drown.'

'Ethan!' said Mum.

'What? That's a nice thing to say. Would have been totally wrong to say I'm sad she didn't.'

Mum rolled her eyes.

'Cheers, Ethan,' I said. 'Love you too.'

Dad called hello from the study before I went upstairs to my room. Mum had obviously taken the chance to clean and de-clutter my room. I dropped onto my bed, which was fresh with clean linen, and got out my phone.

First thing I noticed was my Instagram was getting more likes. I scrolled through a stream of people liking different posts. Loads of people loving the shots and saying it reminded them of going there when they were younger. I was scanning through when I stopped. I double-checked. Scarlett had liked one of my photos, the last one, of me looking out from the end of the pier, the sun setting and the glow warming everything it touched.

Scarlett. What did that mean? Had she forgiven me? Realised the truth?

What should I do with this? I could play it cool. Act like I'd not noticed, or didn't care. I couldn't help myself. I went to Scarlett's Instagram. The pictures of her and Bailey were gone. Just the ones of Zara and Chelsea were still there. Something had clearly happened. But what? Impulsively, I liked her latest post, before putting my phone away to stop myself doing anything else.

CHAPTER 30

It was Monday – doctor's appointment time. Mum drove me there and came in with me. My stomach was churning and I started to look for places to be sick, my mouth sweating saliva. It had been really hard talking to Mum when I got back, but Hattie had insisted. She said embarrassment wasn't a good enough reason not to. And in the end, it had been totally fine. Mum hadn't asked to see, didn't make a thing out of it; she just gave me a massive hug and said she was glad I'd told her. Early this morning, I overheard her on the phone to the doctor, checking the appointment time.

We told the receptionist we were there and sat down. Half of the waiting room was decorated like a pirate ship, with lots of books and toys. The other half was painted a light green, with loads of out-of-date magazines and a tank of fish.

'Jake Atteridge, please,' called a doctor from a side room.

'That's us,' said Mum, squeezing my hand. She was using her forced cheerful voice.

We walked in and I sat on the chair nearest the doctor. Mum sat next to me.

'Good morning,' said the doctor. 'You must be Jake. I'm Doctor Ravji.'

I nodded. I was gripping my hands to try and stop them from shaking. Perhaps I didn't need to know, perhaps I could go home now and forget all about this. I probably imagined the lump. It had probably disappeared overnight and there'd be nothing to see.

'How can I help you?'

I looked at Mum. When I was little, she always used to do the talking, explaining about my sore throats and nasty coughs, but today she just smiled at me and nodded encouragement.

'Right. Well, um, you see...'

How *do* you say it? Agnes wouldn't have this problem – she'd come right out with everything, medical terms, the lot. The thought of Agnes helped.

I cleared my throat. 'Thing is, I found a lump. Three weeks ago. In the shower.'

Doctor Ravji nodded. 'And where was this lump?'

I paused.

'I'm assuming it's somewhere you find embarrassing?'

I nodded.

'How about I have a look? That might be the best thing.'

How, on any planet, would that be the best thing?

'I know it's embarrassing but, from my point of view, I'm looking after your health. It doesn't matter which bit of the human body I'm looking at, I'm checking for signs of disease or infection and seeing how I can help you feel better. I know for you it's really personal but, please, I've seen everything hundreds of times before. Imagine I'm checking your tonsils. It's like that.'

'Yeah, but without my pants on, right?'

Doctor Ravji smiled. 'Exactly. Right. Come on. Let's have a look.'

He pulled a curtain. Mum stayed, thankfully, on the other side. I'd have thought that would have lessened the cringe, but no. While I was taking my things off, Mum took the chance to relate every embarrassing experience she'd ever had at the doctor's. Doctor Ravji put on gloves and I tried to think of something, anything, else. I noticed a crack in the paint that looked like the coastline round Weston. I kept my eyes on the ceiling and tried to keep my mind there too. The examination didn't hurt. At all. It just felt weird.

'OK, thank you. You can pop your trousers back on,' Doctor Ravji said, snapping off his gloves and disappearing round the curtain. I could hear him washing his hands before going back to his desk.

When I was dressed, I pulled back the curtain and went to sit back by Mum. She patted my knee and gave me a tiny smile. I was glad she was there.

Doctor Ravji stopped typing on his computer.

'So, there is definitely a mass that needs investigating. I'm going to refer you to a urologist, a specialist in this area. It's most likely a cyst, but it could also be something more, so we need to get it checked out. Now, I'm going to need some blood tests and a urine sample before you go. The nurse will help with those.'

My head was spinning. Tests, samples, more appointments.

It was something. I hadn't imagined it.

'Do you have any questions?' asked Doctor Ravji.

'Err. No. I don't think so. Thanks.'

'You did the right thing coming to see me,' he said. 'Remember, I'm always here if you have concerns about your treatment, or if you've got questions.'

I nodded. I should have questions. I should have hundreds of them. It's all I'd had for weeks, and now, just when I could ask them, they'd vanished.

Mum was thanking him, but I couldn't listen. I felt like jelly all over. I wanted to get out of there.

After I'd weed in a pot and had two test tubes of blood taken from my arm – I watched that bit – Mum drove me home. Neither of us said very much.

When we got in, I went straight upstairs to my room. I had done it. Did I feel any better? Sort of, I guess. I still didn't have an answer. The doctor's words rang in my mind. 'You did the right thing.'

Suddenly, I felt ravenous. I'd skipped breakfast that morning. I walked to the top of the stairs. I could hear Mum talking on the phone downstairs.

'Yes. He did great. So proud of him.'

She paused.

'Yeah, I know you're wanting to get something booked, but I think leave it for now. We can always get a last-minute deal. Let's see how things go.'

Mum's voice wobbled a bit on the last sentence. She blew her nose.

'No, I'm fine. I'm a bit worried… Thanks. Yes, it's very difficult.'

Mum was right. All we could do now was wait. Wait to see how our lives would go.

Was not knowing worse than knowing the worst? I'd debated this over and over for weeks, and today I had my answer. I wanted to know. Either way. I had to know.

I headed back to my bedroom. I couldn't let Mum see me. She was upset enough already. As I shut the door, the tears came. It could just be a cyst. The doctor had said that, right? It didn't have to be the worst. It could still be all right. Everything could be fine.

My phone pinged.

Hattie: *Hope it went OK.*

I looked at the message. The appointment itself had been OK. It was hard to process needing more tests.

Me: *It was fine actually. Been referred to a*
              specialist, so still not sure what it is.
Hattie: *Here if you want to talk…*
Me: *Thanks.*

I turned the sound off and put it upside down on my desk, then lay on my bed. I'd not said about the headaches and stomach pain. How could I have forgotten? In a few days I'd be able to ask the specialist. A few more days. It felt as good as a few more years. How in the world was I going to survive that long? I wondered if waiting ever killed anyone?

CHAPTER 31

Because of the way Mum's shifts worked, I was home almost a full twenty-four hours before I saw her.

'Well, hello, stranger,' she said, when she got in.

I was no more of a stranger than I was when I left, but I let it go.

'Did you have a good time? What did you do?'

'Yes, it was good. And we did lots of stuff. I kept a diary, if you want to read some extracts.' She couldn't read it all. A girl has to have some secrets.

'How about you tell me the most exciting thing that happened?'

'Oh, that's easy. Saving Hattie from sinking sands and then being rescued by a hovercraft. Did you know hovercrafts are surprisingly loud, considering they're on a cushion of air?'

'Err, what now?' said Mum.

She's not very good at listening.

'Hovercrafts. They're really noisy.'

Mum shook her head. 'No, before that. The bit about sinking sand.'

'Oh, yes. Hattie got stuck. I went to help her and Jake rang 999. Without a doubt, that was the most exciting part of the week.'

'Everyone OK now?'

'Of course.' Duh.

I started walking up the stairs to my bedroom.

'And I saw Rose too.'

'*What?*'

'Rose.' Surely she knew who I meant? How many Roses did she know?

'I mean, how did you see her? What was she doing in Blackpool?'

Ah. My foot was hovering over the next step up.

Mum stood up. 'Why don't you come down? I'll make us both a cup of tea and you can tell me all about it.'

I frowned. There wasn't a lot to tell. And I definitely didn't want to tell her about Blackpool.

'I'll find a packet of biscuits. And we can dunk them.'

Well, that made all the difference. I followed

Mum into the kitchen. She made us some tea, and put the biscuit tin on the table.

'So, start from the beginning, and tell me everything about Rose. Don't leave anything out.'

I dunked my first biscuit. There is an optimum time for dunking. Too short and the biscuit's still crunchy, too long and it plops and slops.

'We actually went to Weston.'

Mum frowned. 'Not Blackpool?'

'No, Weston-super-Mare.'

Mum was still frowning. 'Did you change your plans?'

'No. We always were going to Weston. I didn't tell you because you'd have tried to stop me.'

'And why would I have tried to stop you?' Mum had folded her arms now. Her biscuit was untouched on the table.

'Because you'd tell me to leave Rose alone; that she's old enough to live her own life and we have to give her the space to do that.'

'If you knew that, why did you go?'

'Because you're wrong. She should be at home, with us. You're always telling me that family's the most important thing, so how come it isn't for Rose?'

Mum stopped frowning, but I wasn't sure what her face was saying now.

'Ah, Aggie,' is all she said. Not much to go on there.

'I even took her the job advert I found in the newsagent's on the corner – she could've walked to work. I would've got used to her new routine. I'm sure I could. I just wanted her home. Then she told me it wasn't a temporary job. That it was a permanent one. She's moved to Weston and she's not coming back after a couple of months.'

Mum stretched her hands out across the table near mine.

'I'm sorry, Agnes, that we told you that. It was my idea. I was so worried…' She stopped and swallowed hard. 'I didn't want to upset you while you had your exams.'

'That's what Rose said too.'

'I didn't want you to have more things to deal with. Do you understand?'

'I think so. I do really miss her though. I miss her lasagne; I miss being able to talk to her; I miss the way she stacks the dishwasher.'

'The dishwasher?' Mum frowned momentarily. 'Listen, honey, when things change, it takes some getting used to. And it can be painful. I'm missing Rose too.'

'You are?'

'Yes, of course.' Mum smiled.

'So why didn't you stop her leaving?'

'Because it's what she needs to do. She needs to try out being an adult, and learn things for herself. We're always here for her, if she needs us, but I can't stop her doing what she wants with her life.'

I thought about this.

'So even though it makes us both sad that she's not here, we have to let her go?'

'Sort of. But seeing Rose happy, makes us happy. How did you feel when you saw her? Did she seem like she was having a good time?'

I reached into my pocket and pulled out the napkin Rose had written on.

'She told me everything. About the people she was sharing a house with, and her job and the places she's been.' As I was telling Mum, I could hear Rose's voice, laughing as she said the chippie was even better than at home. 'I think she's having a brilliant time.'

Mum picked up the job advert, which had dropped out of the napkin, and read it. 'You should apply for this. After your exams. Might be a good way to earn a bit of cash for the summer. You could use it to go and see Rose.'

That wasn't a bad idea. I'd already arranged to go the week after my exams finished.

'Maybe, Mum. Now, let's see if you can learn to stack the dishwasher like Rose.'

CHAPTER 32

I was lying on the sofa when the doorbell rang.

'Hattie, can you get that?' called Dad from the study. He was still super-busy with work. Mum had taken Ethan out so Dad could have complete quiet for the day.

I rolled my eyes and went to answer the door.

On the doorstep were Scarlett, Zara and Chelsea.

'Err, hello?' I said.

'Hi,' said Scarlett.

I narrowed my eyes. There had to be a catch.

'You're back then,' said Zara. Interesting. They'd noticed. The Instagram campaign had worked. Jake and Agnes would be stoked.

'Yes,' I said. I had no plans for the day. I could

quite easily go out with them, if they asked, of course. At least they were speaking to me again.

'So, we've been thinking,' said Scarlett. 'We might have jumped to some conclusions. About you.'

I frowned. 'Like what?'

'About Bailey. And the party.'

'So you believe me? That I didn't do anything? It was him.'

Scarlett nodded. 'Turns out he's been kissing more than just you and me.' Her smile was sad.

'I'm sorry to hear that, Scarlett.' Sorry that she was hurting, but not at all surprised that he'd been caught kissing someone else.

'It's fine. I dumped his sorry ass.'

'Do you want to come in?' This was my chance. I could get back in the group and there was still time to do stuff together before school started again. 'We've got to keep it down cos Dad's working, but…'

'Sure,' said Scarlett, and she walked past me into the hall. Zara followed.

'Just go into the kitchen,' I said, waiting for Chelsea. Zara and Scarlett headed off down the hall.

'I never believed it,' said Chelsea quietly, as she

passed me. 'All that stuff with Bailey. Never thought you'd have done it.'

I frowned. She'd blocked and defriended me, just like the others had. But never mind, we'd sorted it out now.

'Thanks, Chelsea,' I said as I shut the door.

'We can't stay long,' said Scarlett. 'We're off shopping this afternoon, then out for Stephanie Brown's birthday tonight.'

I waited a beat to see if I'd get included. I didn't.

'That's nice,' I said.

I could hear Agnes laughing in my head. 'Nice? Sounds horrific!' It made me smile to myself.

'Could I have a drink?' asked Zara. 'Only the mochas when we're out are soooo expensive. And we'd save a ton of money by having one here.'

'Sure.' I got boiling and frothing.

Scarlett had her phone out and was scrolling through pictures, showing them to the other two who were leaning over her shoulder. I poured hot water onto the coffee and stirred all four cups. The three of them broke out into helpless laughter. I looked over.

'What?'

'Oh, nothing. It's just this guy. You don't know him. He's just *so funny*.' More laughing.

I topped each coffee with a floating island of frothy milk and carried them over to the table where they were sitting.

'Cheers,' said Zara, without looking up. Scarlett found another picture and there was more laughing.

'Oh, Hattie?' said Chelsea.

'Yes?' I could almost hear the hope and desperation in my voice and cringed.

'You got any of those chocolate shakes to put on top?'

As I rummaged in the cupboard, I could hear Jake now. 'They don't sound much like friends to me.'

Stop thinking like that. I shook myself. It was going to take time to feel comfortable in their company again. I'd spent so much time with Agnes and Jake, I was starting to think like them. This type of friendship didn't work like that. This took more work, but would be worth it.

I gave Chelsea the shaker and she shook it so much the whole table was covered in chocolate powder. With a sinking feeling, I knew there was no way she'd clear it up.

We drank our mochas, them laughing over stuff I knew nothing about, and me hating myself for laughing along.

It was a relief when Scarlett declared it was time for them to leave.

'So glad you're back, Hattie,' she said. Her smile reached to about her cheekbones.

The other two smiled, the same tight-lipped smile. Mum's name for them echoed around my head. 'Unholy trinity.' I grinned.

'What's so funny?' asked Scarlett, now in a slightly better mood.

'Oh nothing. Just pleased to be back with my mates.'

'Relatable,' said Zara.

'Hattie, can we leave our change of clothes for Stephanie's party here? It would save us carrying them around the shops. You wouldn't mind, would you?'

'No. That's fine.'

They heaped a pile of bags under the hall table. I stood, leaning on the door frame as the three of them walked down our drive.

'See you around,' Chelsea called back.

I pushed the door shut. I'd got what I wanted. We were back together. I was no longer being ghosted, but why did it feel so crap?

Eugh. I kicked the door.

'Quiet!' Dad shouted from the study.

'No, you be quiet!' I yelled back. I stomped up the stairs, making sure I really stamped on each step. I didn't want to be quiet. I flung myself down on my bed. How had it got like this?

There was a knock. I sighed. 'It's all right, Dad. I'll keep the noise down.'

He stuck his head round the door.

'I was wondering, you know, if everything's OK? Realised it's been ages since we've had a proper catch-up. I'm due a break about now – fancy a cuppa?'

'Nah, you're all right, Dad. I know you're busy. I'll sort it out.'

He came into the room and perched on the edge of my bed.

'You know, I work really hard for you and Ethan and your mum. You're like the fuel that keeps me going.'

I smiled at him. 'I know, Dad.'

'But it's all a complete waste of time if I'm not actually there for you.'

I must have looked surprised.

'See?' he said. 'Proof we've not been chatting enough. The very idea of me being there for you is a surprise.' He was smiling, but his eyes looked kind of sad. 'What's going on that's making you kick doors? That's not like you.'

I propped myself up against the headboard.

'Was it the unholy trinity?'

I smiled. Mum must have told him.

'Yeah, they're back talking to me again. They said they've realised I was telling the truth about something.'

'O-K,' said Dad. 'What made them change their minds?'

'Someone else said the same thing. And they believed them, which meant they believed me.'

'I can see why you might kick a door.'

'But they're my friends. I want to be back with them. I do…'

'How do they make you feel better about yourself? Because friendship is a two-way street. It's always worth a check – what do I do to help my friends, but equally, what do they do for me? It's tough, but it's got to be both. And sometimes it's more one than the other if there's a crisis, or someone's going through tough times. But if it's always one-sided, you've got to question it.'

I wanted to shout that he was wrong. These guys were my friends – they always had been.

'If you find someone who will put themselves out for you, you hang on to them. Those sorts of friends don't come along all that often.'

I hesitated.

'The sort that would walk into sinking sand to save you? The sort that would go all out to make you laugh, even if they were feeling ill and scared?'

Dad looked confused.

'Never mind. Yeah. I've got the best kind of friends. Just not any of that lot.'

He smiled, clearly totally not getting what I was talking about.

'You know what? I will have a cuppa.'

Dad really smiled then. 'And I know where the secret stash of biscuits is too.'

I hugged him tight and he kissed the top of my head.

'You make me more proud each day, you know that?'

'Yeah, but no harm in saying it again.' I grinned.

When the doorbell rang later that afternoon, I was ready.

I opened the door. 'Hi,' I said to Zara, Chelsea and Scarlett.

They looked surprised. It must have been the wide, confident smile.

'Err, hello?' said Zara. 'We popped by for our bags.'

'And we wondered if we could get changed here too.' Scarlett stepped forward.

'Oh, I'm sorry. You can have your bags, but you can't change here.'

'Really?' Her eyebrows arched.

'Yeah. You all claimed I'd lied to you. And kissed your boyfriend.' I looked right at Scarlett. 'You all were totally fine assuming that. Even though I told you it wasn't what happened. You took random Sharleen's word for it.'

They all looked shocked.

'Which sucks a bit, right?'

Nothing.

'So this friendship is over. It was over the moment you didn't believe me. The moment you didn't stick up for your friend. The moment you thought I was capable of doing something like that. We can't move on from that. So please, collect your bags and leave.'

'What?' said Chelsea. 'What are you on about?'

'Thanks very much, but no thanks. I've got people who'll treat me better than this.'

Zara laughed. 'No, you haven't. There's no one else you're friends with. You know everyone through us, and when they find out what you've said, no one will ever speak to you again.'

My hands were shaking. This threat usually worked. Usually had me backing down. Usually had me feeling like crap. I thought about Agnes and Jake. They wouldn't stop speaking to me.

'So what? If they believe you over me, then they're not my friends either.'

'Come on, let's get out of here,' said Scarlett, grabbing her bag before turning on her heel and storming off down our drive.

I smiled a big wide smile at Chelsea and Zara. 'See you around.'

As soon as they were out, I shut the door behind them, letting the latch quietly click shut.

Dad was clapping from the study. I stuck my head round the door. He was sitting at his desk, beaming.

'Well done! How do you feel?'

'Shaky. But good, I think.'

Dad nodded. 'You've done one of the hardest things in life. And the next time you find yourself with people like that, you'll spot them sooner, and get out faster.'

'Thanks, Dad,' I said. I left him to his work and headed back up to my room. Once stretched out on my bed, I pulled out my phone. My hands were still shaking but I knew what I wanted to do. My

Instagram needed a makeover. I deleted all my posts. Time for a completely fresh start.

I uploaded shot after shot and, when I was finished, I looked back over them. One of me and Jake in the early morning sunshine, him pulling a face, me with my 'I ❤ Weston' hat on; another of me and Agnes both wrapped in blankets sitting in A&E; one of me screaming with laughter as I tried to get pink candyfloss out of my hair. The last shot was of Jake, Agnes and me, leaning against the sea wall, all laughing in the sunshine. I looked at it and smiled.

CHAPTER 33

Jake

My phone never pings. Not since I was taken off the team's group chat. So it was a surprise when my phone buzzed so much that it walked its way to the edge of the table and fell off into my pile of clothes.

I checked it. Loads and loads of Instagram notifications. And still going. I clicked on one. A picture of me and Agnes both looking out to sea. But Agnes hadn't posted it. Hattie had. I read the caption. 'The best friends a person could wish for.'

She'd obviously lost the plot. This would destroy her chances of getting back with her mates. If she deleted them quickly, perhaps they wouldn't notice.

Me: *Stop posting on Instagram!*
Hattie: *Why? Don't you like my pictures?*

Me: *Your mates are going to go mental.*

Hattie: *If you mean those other three, they're not my mates.*

Me: *Huh?*

Hattie: *I've had an epiphany.*

Me: *Was it painful?*

Agnes: *I think you might be confused, Jake. An epiphany is an enlightenment, not something that causes physical pain.*

Me: *Thanks A, lol.*

Agnes: *You're welcome.*

Hattie: *Dad's said he's going to cook tonight. And he's said I can invite some friends if I want. Think all the work has gone to his head. It's like he's on holiday. Do you both want to come over?*

Agnes: *Maybe. What's he cooking?*

Me: *Yeah, sounds good.*

Hattie: *His signature dish. Whatever he can find in the fridge, all in together. Usually pretty good. Only once been a massive failure. (Mackerel. Nasty.)*

Agnes: *I will risk it.*

Mum was fine with letting me go. There was no way she was going to say anything other than yes. Unexpected perk of possibly being seriously ill.

I rang the doorbell and waited. Agnes came running up the street.

'Mum found out about Blackpool,' she said as she got to me.

'How come?'

'I accidently mentioned Rose.' She pulled a face.

'Ouch.' I laughed.

'I don't know why you're laughing. Hattie's family don't even know you went to Weston!'

That made me laugh harder. This was going to be an interesting evening.

Hattie opened the door. She was wearing her usual jeans and a much bigger than normal smile.

'Come in,' she said. 'Dad's having a culinary crisis, so Mum's trying to help without being seen to help. It's hilarious.'

We followed her along the hallway to a big, brightly-lit kitchen. Her dad was stirring something vigorously in a massive wok. Her mum was washing up, but stopped when we came in. Her eyes took in both me and Agnes. She smiled.

'Hello. You must be Agnes, lovely to meet you, and Jake, is it? Nice to meet you, too. Tea shouldn't be long. Grab yourself a drink. Hattie, can you help them?'

Hattie's dad waved a spatula in our direction.

'Hey, guys, not long now. And if I do say so myself, tonight's meal is going to be a masterpiece.'

'No mackerel?' asked Agnes.

Hattie's dad laughed. 'You've heard the legend, then?'

Agnes went to inspect the contents of the wok. Clearly she was unsure about his culinary offerings.

I spotted Hattie's brother in the corner, plugged into his Xbox. I walked over to see what he was playing.

'Hey,' I said.

'Hey,' he said back.

'What level you got to?'

'Level 12.'

'What? That's insane. I've been playing every waking hour and only got level 10 yesterday.'

'I can give you some hacks, if you like?'

'Seriously? That would be awesome.'

Hattie came over.

'I didn't know you were a gamer,' she said, bumping my arm.

'Ah, I'm full of hidden talents.' I grinned.

'I'd hardly call it a talent.' She smiled.

'Well, what I have perhaps isn't, but your brother's seriously gifted.'

'Yeah, gifted in annoying,' she said, twanging his headphones on his head.

I wished I had a brother or sister. It looked fun to have someone to hang out with. Then Ethan tried to punch Hattie back, and I changed my mind. Perhaps being an only child wasn't so bad.

'OK, tea's ready,' said Hattie's dad. 'Sit wherever you like, and it's stretch or starve.'

We crowded around the table, wok steaming in the centre with extra dishes containing rice, naan breads and pickles circling it. It smelled amazing.

'So, Jake,' said Hattie's mum, once we'd all piled our plates with food. 'I hear from Hattie that you went to Weston too?'

Hattie was grinning. She'd sorted that problem out. I caught Agnes smiling.

'Yes, that's right. A really brilliant study break.'

Ethan nearly choked on his food.

'Well...' His mum shot him a stern look. 'Hattie's dad and I are very grateful for what you and Agnes did that day on the beach. Hattie told us all about it, and so did Sadie. Thank you so much.'

I could feel my blush rising. 'No problem. It's what friends do. Right, Agnes?'

'Right,' she said.

It wasn't until much, much later that evening when I was lying in bed that I remembered. Tomorrow. Hospital. Appointment booked for two-forty. I shut my eyes and tried to put it out of my head. I couldn't change what it was. It was already decided. The universe already knew which way this would play. I didn't know yet, that's all. Wouldn't change by me knowing.

I sighed and went back to Hattie's Instagram. Dozens of pictures of me and Hattie and Agnes scrolled past. The one of us playing the two-penny machines, the candyfloss, Agnes' first ride on a donkey and, finally, the one of the three of us, laughing our heads off. I smiled.

The knot of nerves was still chewing away at my insides. I would not crumble. I would not let whatever this was beat me. Tomorrow I might know what was trying to but, until then, I'd just survive.

Another tear joined the other. I was going to fight this, but would my new friends stick with me if things got tough?

CHAPTER 34

It was a big day. The first time ever, in the history of my life, I was meeting up with a friend in town. A friend. Mum said I'd been saying 'meeting a friend in town' to myself all morning. I told her I just liked the way it sounded. No big deal. No need to make *A Thing* out of it. Though I totally was.

I caught the bus. Hattie was already sitting towards the back.

'Over here, Agnes!' she said, waving her arms at me. The man whose hat she nearly knocked off muttered something.

I walked down the bus and sat beside her. I was so nervous and excited I was nearly twitching.

'What's up with you?' said Hattie.

'Just really excited.'

'What for?'

'Going into town.'

Hattie frowned a little. 'How come? It's only town.'

'Never been into town with a friend before.'

Hattie was quiet. I guessed I'd answered her question, so there was nothing more to say. Then she spoke softly. 'Well, you'd better get used to it. I'm a massive shopaholic and I'm going to need my best mate to tell me when something doesn't suit me.'

Did she mean me? She smiled at me. I think that meant she did.

'Oh, I can *definitely* tell you when something doesn't suit you,' I said. 'Absolutely no problem with that.'

Hattie laughed. 'Perfect! So, where first?'

We shopped and shopped before finally ending up with milkshakes and burgers on a bench outside Topshop.

'Shopping is an endurance sport,' I said, as I wriggled my aching toes in my trainers. 'You do training for this, right?'

Hattie laughed. 'No! This *is* the training. The real sport is the sales.'

I groaned and Hattie laughed again.

I looked at my watch. It was two-thirty. 'I

wonder how Jake's getting on.' We'd sent him pictures of us all morning and he'd replied, but we knew he'd be on the way to the hospital now.

'Did he sound nervous to you?' asked Hattie.

I thought. I wasn't sure exactly what nervous would sound like.

'He said the doctor's was OK,' Hattie said. 'It didn't hurt or anything, just felt really odd.'

I frowned. 'Some experts think having people to support you helps. I read it on a website. It can help the patient feel more positive and calm. Do you think that's true?'

Hattie was nodding. 'Definitely.'

'Do you think we should be Jake's people? His support people?'

Hattie chewed her nail. 'I keep thinking, what would I want people to do for me, if it was me in Jake's shoes? And I don't know.'

'The website said that it was very important. I think we should.'

Hattie nodded again. 'And if he doesn't want us there, he only has to say, and we'll go. Agreed?'

'Agreed.'

'Where's his appointment?'

'Hospital. Down the road. I reckon we can make it if we run.'

'Run?' said Hattie.

I grinned. 'You've been in training all morning. Let's go!'

We ran down the high street, under the dual carriageway, down several walkways and paths until we got to the huge hospital.

'Where now?' said Hattie, panting.

I found the map on the wall. I ran my finger down the lists of departments. 'Got it. Not far now.'

We ran again, this time along corridors and up stairs, our trainers squeaking on the shiny lino. We arrived at a small, quiet waiting room very out of breath.

There was no one in there. A lady behind a glass screen looked at us.

'Excuse me, we're looking for Jake Atteridge,' Hattie panted.

'And you are?' said the lady.

'His friends,' I said. 'It's very important. We're here to support him.'

The lady smiled. 'If you wait here, he shouldn't be long.'

We sat down, sweating and out of breath. The handles of all the bags were cutting into my fingers, so I tucked them under my seat.

Suddenly, a door banged open and Jake shot

out. He ran through the waiting room and out into the corridor.

A woman, who I recognised from the train station as Jake's mum, came out after him, her face all screwed up, like she'd stubbed her toe or something.

Hattie immediately jumped up. 'Where did Jake go?'

His mum looked confused. I supposed she didn't know who we were. A doctor came out of the room behind her.

'Who are you?' she asked us.

'We're Jake's support team,' I said.

Hattie was looking from one woman to the other. 'Shall I go after him?'

His mum nodded and then slumped onto a chair. Hattie shot off out of the room and I could hear her trainers squeaking away as she ran after Jake.

I looked at the doctor and then at Jake's mum. I never know what to say in these situations. I just know it's very important to say the right thing. But what is the right thing? I flicked through a dozen options but none sounded right, and instead I ended up doing what everyone agrees is pretty bad. Freezing and not saying anything at all.

CHAPTER 35

Hattie

I didn't see which way Jake went, so I guessed and ran back along the corridors me and Agnes had run along a few minutes before. I got to the main door and shot through it. Which way now? I looked both ways and spotted him. On a bench. No need to run anymore.

I walked over to him.

'Hey,' I said. He looked up at me, surprised. His face was blotchy and he was crying.

'What are you doing here?'

I sat down next to him.

'Agnes' idea. She reckoned we needed to be your support crew.'

He didn't say anything.

'You OK?' I asked, knowing he clearly wasn't.

'What do you reckon?' It wasn't said unkindly.

'Want to tell me?'

He shook his head. 'I heard everything the doctor said, and then everything went strange. Like I was watching my life as a movie. And my mum was sat there, holding her breath and gripping her bag so tightly. And I couldn't listen anymore. I don't want to hear it. I've changed my mind. I don't want to know.'

He was breathing deeply, trying hard to hold the tears back.

I waited, letting my arm rest against his.

'They said it's cancer. I knew it was. I knew it. It's got a fancy name. I didn't catch it. The doctor was saying stuff about stages and treatments and prognosis and a ton of other stuff and I was hearing it and not hearing it at the same time. And then I ran. Not entirely sure that's the most sensible thing I've ever done, to be honest. Not like I can run away from it.'

'Understandable, though, to want to try.'

He wiped his eyes on the short sleeve of his T-shirt and sniffed.

'I don't think I can do this.'

'What?'

'The whole cancer thing. It's going to change everything.'

'Yeah, probably.'

'And everyone will know and talk about me.'

'Maybe.'

'And,' his voice dropped, 'what if my friends don't stick around.'

'The good ones will. And you've met Agnes, right? She's absolutely going nowhere. She's made up her mind.'

He looked at me, his eyes bloodshot from crying.

'And I'm right there too. Every step. By the end of this, you'll be sick of the sight of us. You'll be begging to have a break from us.'

Jake smiled weakly. 'I'll make sure I say, if that ever happens.'

We sat in silence for a few moments more, the evidence of the tears gradually fading.

'You ready to go back?' I asked.

He nodded. 'Let's get this over with. Or started with.'

I linked my arm through his and we walked back in through the big doors of the hospital.

'Oh, thank goodness.' Jake's mother flung her arms around him as soon as he stepped inside the waiting room. Agnes was at the other end of the room, and the doctor was standing in the doorway to her office.

'All right, Jake?' she asked. 'Ready to come back in?'

He nodded.

'We're coming too,' said Agnes, stepping forward.

I felt a bit weird about pushing ourselves forward. Even though I'd just said we'd be there for him, perhaps that wasn't for the actual appointments. This was a super-private thing. Perhaps Jake wouldn't want us there. Perhaps his mum wouldn't either.

'That's up to Jake and his mum,' said the doctor, looking to them for guidance.

Jake looked at Agnes, who was looking fiercely determined. Then he looked at me, a question in his eyebrows.

'Right there,' I said, 'if you want us?'

He nodded the tiniest of nods. His mum continued to look utterly confused.

Agnes stepped forward and held her hand out. 'I'm Agnes, and this is Hattie. We're Jake's friends.' She fished in one of the bags, pulled out a bottle of water and handed it to Jake. 'Best to stay hydrated. Tears can be very drying.'

Jake took the bottle. 'Thanks, Agnes.'

Agnes nodded an acknowledgement, then pulled out a new pad and pen she'd bought that morning.

'OK, Jake, ready when you are.'

Jake shook his head. A watery smile appeared for a split second before he walked back into the doctor's office, his mum following, with me and Agnes last.

I sat the other side of Jake from his mum. Agnes dragged in an extra chair and sat right by the doctor, notepad and pen at the ready.

'As I was saying, it looks very likely you have testicular cancer. It's a type of cancer which is highly treatable, and the prognosis is excellent. It looks like we've caught it in the early stages, and we'll do a few more tests to confirm this.'

'What treatments are you recommending, doctor?' said Agnes, who had been scribbling furiously in her notepad.

'It's surgery.'

I saw Jake tense up.

'It's a simple, easy procedure, done under general anaesthetic, but we like to do it quickly. The worry with cancer is that it can spread. It doesn't look like yours has, Jake, and we want to keep it that way.'

He was listening, but kept zoning out a bit. I suppose it was a lot of information to take in.

Agnes chewed the end of her pen. 'You don't think it's spread? But Jake's been having other symptoms. Headaches, I think,' she looked to Jake to check.

Jake seemed to wake up at that question. 'Yes, awful headaches and a pain in my stomach. That means it's spread, doesn't it?'

I noticed Jake's mum's knuckles were bleached white, gripping her bag.

'You've not mentioned those before, have you?' said the doctor, looking back over her notes.

'No. I forgot.'

'Tell me a little bit more about them,' said the doctor. 'When did they first start? Have you noticed any pattern to them?'

Jake thought hard. 'It's only been the last few weeks, and they're usually worst at night or when I'm by myself with nothing going on.'

The doctor nodded and made some notes. 'Would you say they started before or after you found the lump?'

Jake thought again. 'After.'

Agnes was writing down every word.

'I think Jake that they may be anxiety-related.

The pressure of finding a lump and thinking in circles about what that could mean. Is that something you've found yourself doing?'

Jake nodded, his nose flaring as he struggled to hold back the tears. 'Yes. I can't stop thinking about it. All the time. I've been trying to find other things to do and think about, but it doesn't work when I'm on my own.'

'It's really common, Jake.'

'So, it doesn't mean the cancer has spread?'

She shook her head. 'We'll check, of course, but I'm certain we've caught your cancer in the very early stages, and the pains in your head and stomach are your body's response to the stress of finding a lump.'

A tear ran down Jake's cheek.

Agnes broke off from writing to rummage in her bag. She pulled out a tissue and handed it to Jake.

Jake's mum asked a question.

'He's got exams in a few weeks. His GCSEs.'

'I'd like to do the surgery next week, and it's usually a couple of weeks of recovery, so he should be well enough to take his exams.'

'That is brilliant news,' said Agnes.

Jake blew his nose. 'You mean I can have cancer,

and I still don't get out of doing my exams? Life really isn't fair.'

Everyone laughed. But it was nervous laughter. The kind that feels all out of place but you can't help.

The doctor explained the operation and recovery expectations, and gave some more facts and figures which Agnes wrote down, her pen flying across the pages of her notebook. She wasn't going to suffer from hand cramps in her English exam.

Once Agnes had asked all her questions, and Jake had had some more blood taken, we found ourselves back at the main entrance of the hospital.

'Well, I don't know about anyone else, but I could murder a cuppa,' said Jake's mum. 'Agnes, Hattie, do you fancy joining us?'

'Can I have a mocha and a satsuma, please?' asked Agnes. 'It is Friday.'

'Of course,' said Jake's mum, frowning a bit. Jake was smiling.

We found a nearly clean table in the hospital café and sat there while Jake's mum went to the toilet.

Agnes sipped her mocha as she read back over her notes. 'It's not a bad diagnosis.'

Jake and I looked at her in surprise.

'What do you mean?' said Jake.

'It could have been a lot worse.' She looked up from her notes and saw our faces. 'What? You even thought it was.'

Jake nodded. 'I did. Still, finding it hard to see the upside exactly.'

'Really? But it could have been all sorts.' She reeled off a list of impressive sounding diseases. 'But you haven't got those. You've got this. At stage one as well. If you had to have something, this is not a bad one.'

'Easy for you to say,' muttered Jake.

'Well, I'm hugely relieved,' said Agnes. 'I wasn't about to lose one of the only two friends I've ever had.'

That shut Jake up. He sipped his tea, the steam obviously being the thing that was making his eyes water.

I wanted to change the subject, but everything seemed to be coloured by Jake's illness. What are we going to do over the summer? Depends on his treatment. Have you revised for our first exam? I'm just adding more stress. Did you see that program last night? How can I move on from this so quickly?

I decided to sip my drink.

It was Agnes who broke the silence.

'I think we need to do something this weekend.' She looked at me. 'Something fun, something non-stressful, and something that doesn't prevent us from doing some revision first.'

'I'm not sure,' said Jake.

'It says that talking is good for you, but distraction is too. Give your brain a rest from thinking about it. You said that helped your headaches. How about the cinema? We could get chips after.'

You know, she wasn't wrong. She was going at this like a bull at a gate, but maybe that was the way to be. Really honest. I thought about trying to say something supportive, but I didn't know what that would sound like.

His mum came back and the conversation moved on. She asked me and Agnes questions, as if she wasn't ready to face up to what had happened this afternoon either. Jake's mind was clearly not on the conversation, as he picked away at his biscuit wrapper, flattening it, then folding it and then turning it over and over in his fingers.

'Thanks for coming today,' he said suddenly. 'It was all getting a bit heavy. And well, it is big stuff and everything. But you've made it easier somehow.'

Agnes beamed. 'See,' she said to me.

His mum squeezed his hand. I think she was pleased we were there.

CHAPTER 36

Jake

When I woke up the next morning, the sun was coming through the crack in the curtains, and I could hear from the general noise outside that it wasn't early morning. I stretched a bit, then remembered, and the warm sleepy feeling vanished, replaced by a cold, shuddering fear. The questions I'd been blocking out came rushing into my head. How long's the treatment going to take? How ill would I feel? Would I still be able to do stuff?

And the big one: what if it doesn't work?

That's the one that stayed the longest, circling round my brain, along with variations of: will I always be expecting it to come back? Is my life now effectively over?

I didn't want to feel like this, I didn't want to

spend my time thinking this, but how could I stop it? How did I could my brain off? Getting stressed by it, surely, would make everything worse.

I sat up, hoping to throw my brain out of its funk, and picked up my phone. I'd been spammed with texts from Hattie and Agnes. Ten minutes later, when I'd finished reading them all, I realised I'd not thought about *It* the whole time. Perhaps Agnes was right. Perhaps finding things to distract me was the way to give my brain a break. Not ignoring it, just choosing not to think about it the whole time. Or something.

Me: *So, I've been thinking…*
Hattie: *Careful*
Me: *Ha! I reckon the cinema tonight is a good idea. Fancy going still?*
Hattie: *Yep*
Agnes: *Absolutely.*

We arranged to meet up, then I headed downstairs. I needed breakfast.

Mum sat at the kitchen table, a cold mug of tea in front of her.

'You OK, Mum?'

She jumped.

'Sorry, didn't hear you come down. How you feeling?'

'OK, I think. Hard to tell. It's all a bit sudden, you know?'

Mum nodded.

'But as Agnes keeps reminding me, the odds are good.'

Mum's smile nearly slipped. 'Yes. Very good. Excellent, the doctor said, didn't she?'

I started getting my breakfast. 'I'm going out this evening.'

'Oh, that's good,' said Mum. 'Where are you going?'

'Cinema. With Agnes and Hattie. Then we're going for chips. Agnes says she knows the best place this side of Manchester.'

Mum laughed. 'Agnes is funny. Brilliantly direct. And Hattie's lovely too.'

'Yeah,' I said, 'they're great. They're kind of getting me through it.'

Mum nodded. 'I can tell.'

I sat down next to Mum, with my breakfast. 'Who's getting you through this, Mum?'

'What do you mean?'

'Surely the only thing worse than having cancer, is your kid having cancer.'

I think I must have caught her off guard. It took her moment or two before she could speak.

'You. You being such an amazing young man.'

'That's wonderful, Mum, thanks. But you need to tell your friends. I know I said I didn't want loads of people knowing, but you need your mates. People to talk to rather than sitting here, letting your tea go cold.'

Mum hugged me.

'And Mum? I'm sorry I've been snapping. I didn't mean to.'

'That's OK. When you're worried or stressed, it can come out like that. You know, you can always talk to me. About anything. And I'm so, so pleased you talked to me about this.'

I met up with Hattie and Agnes at the big cinema in town. We hadn't completely decided which film we were going to watch. Hattie wanted a rom-com, I fancied the latest Marvel one and Agnes wanted the Disney remake.

'How are we going to pick?' I asked.

'I think you should pick, Jake,' said Hattie.

Agnes frowned. 'Why?'

'Well, because, you know, he's having a tough time, and if we're supposed to be taking his mind off "things", he should pick.'

'You can say the word cancer, you know,' I said. 'It's not like Voldemort.'

'It feels a bit weird, saying it, though. Especially as we're not supposed to be thinking about it all.'

'How about … you can talk about it if you want to, and not if you don't.'

'Sounds good,' said Hattie.

'Well, I don't mind saying it,' said Agnes. 'Besides, it was my idea to come to the cinema, so I should pick. You don't get to play the cancer card, Jake.'

Hattie snorted and I laughed too.

'Disney it is, then,' I said.

After the movie, we went to the chippy Agnes had been raving about. Turns out she's got a whole system for rating chip shops – portion size, greasiness, squidgy/crispy ratio, if there's free sauce. It was a takeaway but had a couple of tables round the back overlooking the car park. It wasn't quite dark and not too cold either.

We sat around our shared, large portion of chips, a puddle of ketchup to one side.

'Nice choice of film, Agnes,' said Hattie.

'And great chips too,' I said, through a mouthful of the nicest chips I'd ever tasted.

'If you do your research, you're not disappointed.'

Agnes wiped a chip through a drip of vinegar on the paper.

We sat eating for a bit.

'The hospital rang this morning,' I said.

'Oh?' said Hattie. 'What did they want?'

'They've set a date for my operation. It's Wednesday.'

'It's good it's so soon,' said Agnes. 'Odds-wise.'

'Quite quick to get your head round, though?' asked Hattie.

I shrugged. It all felt so new and strange that it was tricky to know what I thought.

'Do you have to get there really early?' asked Agnes. 'You usually do with operations.'

I nodded. 'No lie-in that day.'

'Do you want us to come with you?' Hattie asked.

'Because we absolutely will do,' said Agnes.

I laughed. The idea of them being at the hospital with me made me smile.

'No, I'll be fine. Honestly. Mum'll be there. And, besides, you can't miss school. Your parents would go nuts. You've got exams coming up.'

'True,' Hattie nodded.

'Funny how my mum is now surprisingly chill about me missing school,' I grinned.

'Bit extreme, though, don't you reckon, just to get a couple of weeks off school?' said Hattie.

'I think I'm going to miss going to school.' Agnes sighed.

'Really?' I said.

Agnes shrugged. 'I like knowing how each day is going to work.'

'You should get a job,' I said. 'Then you'd get some structure. I read somewhere that having structure helps.'

'You read somewhere?'

My face warmed. 'I wanted to understand, what it's like, I mean. So I googled Asperger's. You don't mind, do you? Only you've helped me so much. I don't know, I just wanted to return the favour.'

'No, that's fine,' said Agnes. 'What did you learn?'

'Loads.' She didn't sound like she minded. 'That people are neurotypical or neurodivergent, which honestly sounds like some kick-ass Marvel character.'

Agnes laughed. 'Yeah, and honesty is my super-power.'

'But, seriously, a job might be good.'

'And you'd get some money,' Hattie added.

Agnes thought for a bit. 'The money would come in handy now I have a friend who likes shopping.'

Hattie grinned. 'What can I say? It's my calling.'

'What are you both going to do after your exams?' Agnes asked.

Hattie shrugged. 'A-levels. I've got a place at college to do geography, art and psychology. Depending on results, of course.' She pulled a face. 'What about you, Jake?'

We'd finished the chips so we pushed back our chairs and started to walk home.

'I'd thought an apprenticeship somewhere. Though I can't seem to think that far ahead to be honest. Can't really see past my operation.'

'Understandable,' said Hattie.

'How's the revision going?' asked Agnes.

'Revision?' said Hattie. 'Not started. I've still got loads of time.'

'I'm planning to do it all while I'm stuck at home recovering,' I said.

Agnes sighed. 'Do you need me to do personalised revision timetables for you both?'

Hattie laughed. 'Nah, I'm just going to wing it. It'll be fine.'

'No way!' I said. 'Just make sure you come and visit me instead, OK?'

'OK,' said Agnes, and grinned.

CHAPTER 37

3 weeks later

When I got onto the bus to school for our first GCSE exam, I was expecting all the year elevens to be quietly revising. I was wrong.

Jake and Hattie were already there. I walked down the aisle and slid into my usual seat.

'All right?' said Jake, peering between the headrests.

'I am,' I said. 'Revision completed. I'm ready. How about you?'

Hattie laughed. 'I'm going for the "wing it and hope" option with this one. Still got time to revise for the later ones.'

'I've read through some of my notes,' said Jake. 'But, yeah, not hopeful.'

At the next stop, another group of kids got on. Ben stopped by Jake on his way past.

'You're back? That's brilliant,' he said.

'Yeah, hi,' said Jake.

'Look, I'm sorry I didn't get why you stopped playing,' Ben said.

'No worries,' said Jake. 'I didn't exactly explain it well.'

Ben smiled. 'Even so, I'm sorry. We're having an end of exams party in a few weeks. I'll add you back into the group chat, so you get to hear the details. I only took you off cos I thought you wanted to concentrate on your exams and I didn't want to distract you. Would be great if you could make it.'

'Sure, thanks,' said Jake. I sneaked a look back at them. Jake was smiling.

'So, how's things? Cancer-wise?' Ben asked.

'Good. Really good. The operation was a success and they don't think it's spread.'

'That's great news, man.'

I wondered if friends were like sisters; you have to let them go and then be happy when they're happy. Was Jake getting back with his old friends and going to leave me and Hattie?

Jake's face appeared again between the headrests.

'So, what's the plan for the weekend?'

'Duh,' I said. 'Revision, obviously.'

'You can't revise all the time, Agnes,' said Hattie, grinning. 'You'll burn out.'

She was teasing me. That's what friends do to show they care. 'OK, something else as well as revision then.'

'You're on,' said Hattie. 'But you don't get to pick this time.'

Jake smiled. 'I've got a feeling it's going to be a Very Good Summer.'

A NOTE FROM KATE...

Although *Asking for a Friend* is fiction it does contain some issues that affect young people. The statistics on the number of young people who experience social bullying, for example, is more than half, so you or a friend is likely to know how this feels.

With anything that's worrying you, find an adult you trust (parent, relative, teacher, friendly dinner lady) and talk to them. Take a friend with you for support, if you want. Tell them. They can help, even if you can't see how.

If you are worried about your health – if you've got something that's unexpected or unexplained – go to your doctor. Get it checked out.

If any aspect of this story has felt personal, here are a few places to start looking for help and information:

National Autistic Society – the UK's leading organisation working towards a society that works for autistic people. This site is packed with useful, easy-to-use information.

www.autism.org.uk

Bullying UK – this website gives advice, to both young people and adults, about all areas of family life. One of these sections is about bullying. It's worth checking out.

www.bullying.co.uk/advice-for-young-people/

Teenage Cancer Trust – these people are awesome. They provide specialist advice and medical care to teens and young adults with cancer. They get what it's like.

www.teenagecancertrust.org

ACKNOWLEDGEMENTS

Firstly, huge thanks to my agent Hannah Sheppard, who has brainstormed, advised and reassured. I love working with you.

Thanks also to the fabulous Firefly Press team, but especially Janet Thomas, my editor, Meg Farr and Simone Greenwood for getting my books out there, and to Anne Glenn for another stunning cover. I'm thrilled you took me on for a second book.

Thank you to Inclusive Minds and Ella Sanderson for your advice. If there are mistakes, they are mine. Thank you to Gilly McAllister for coming up with a killer title when I'd been stuck for months, you are a genius!

Thanks to all my writers' groups, on and off-line: AWC, the Vine Writers, the Doomsday Writers, the Swag crew, the debuts of 2019, SCBWI and fellow students on the Writing for Young People MA course at Bath Spa University. Your combined wealth of knowledge is awesome and your love and understanding makes me feel lucky to know you all.

Thank you to all the lovely, passionate people

who put my books into the hands of readers. I have met so many amazing librarians, teachers, bloggers and booksellers this past year – thank you from the bottom of my heart.

To all the people who have cheered me on, but especially Tizzie Frankish, Tae Carpenter, Az Dassu, Debra Bertulis and Emma Finlayson-Palmer. Thank you for being there. A very special thank you to Zoe Cookson for reading, suggesting and encouraging. You have no idea how much your kind words have helped.

To my family and friends, for supporting and buying in bulk, thank you!

Mark, Sophie, Rory, Noah and Tilda – I love you.

And to you, my reader. Thank you for trusting me with your time.